T0306922

TAILs:

THE ANIMAL INVESTIGATORS OF LONDON

Yowl is a very special tabby kitten owned by 6-year-old Lucy. Sitting on her lap through endless children's books, he learns to read. From the local paper, he discovers there's a criminal on the loose in Croydon targeting cats. TV news reports confirm over seventy incidents. With the help of his feline neighbours, he enlists the support of Big Red, the leader of the foxes, to hunt down the killer. Secret, a squirrel who's afraid of heights, will play a crucial role, but it's Hewt the owl whose help they need most. An eye in the sky will prove essential in identifying the culprit. Yowl will be forced to risk his life to earn his assistance.

Just as they're making progress, the police close the case. They point the finger firmly in the direction of the foxes. In response, Big Red steps up their involvement. Together, they identify the killer, but what can they do to stop him?

TAILS

THE ANIMAL INVESTIGATORS OF LONDON

By Martin Penny

B G S P

First published in 2022
by the Black Spring Press Group
Grantully Road, Maida Vale, London W9,
United Kingdom

Cover art by MJ Hiblen
Typeset by Edwin Smet

ISBN 978-1-913606-49-7

PRINTED IN THE UNITED STATES OF AMERICA
PAPERBACK EDITION

BLACKSPRINGPRESSGROUP.COM

Martin Penny
was born in England and now lives in Turkey, with his wife and children. His father worked on *The Goon Show*. He is an avid book collector of first edition Agatha Christies.

Publisher's note:

This book is based on a true crime story that occurred over several years in and around Croydon, London, beginning in 2010.

While the story may be unsettling, it reminds us how important it is to look after animals, and respect all life.

This book is dedicated to the animal friends we have known and loved throughout our lives.

No animals were harmed in the writing of this book.

Preface

In 2015 South Norwood Animal Rescue and Liberty (SNARL) raised serious concerns with the Metropolitan Police following the discovery of a large number of dead cats. In December 2015, the police launched Operation Takahe in response. It was soon revealed that the initial attacks dated as far back as 2010.

SNARL maintained that a single perpetrator was responsible for the deaths of hundreds of cats. At one point, a £10,000 reward was offered for information leading to the culprit's apprehension. There was even a description of the man given by witnesses: *a white man in his forties with short brown hair, dressed in dark clothing, possibly with acne scarring to his face. He may be wearing a head-lamp or carrying a torch.*

After an investigation lasting three years, the police issued a statement: *No evidence of human involvement was found in any of the reported cases...* They clarified their position on Twitter, suggesting that the cats had been victims of vehicle collisions, with scavenging foxes responsible for the condition of the remains.

SNARL and local residents remain convinced that a human was responsible.

The mystery continues.

1

A Rose by Any Other Name

My name's Yowl.

It's an unfortunate name: a direct result of the anguish I experienced as a kitten when forcibly separated from my mother before my eyes had even opened. Under the same circumstances, you'd probably yowl too.

I never learned what happened to my mother. All I can remember was nuzzling up against her, enjoying her warmth and filling my stomach. When I was full, I tottered away, but not too far. I yowled when she left and I yowled when she didn't come back. I was lucky though: all my yowling attracted the attention of a human. She found me under a bush, picked me up and held me against her chest. I felt safe again. Having spent some time searching for my mother, she took me home. I've been with her ever since.

There were so many unfamiliar scents I had to grow accustomed to: not easy when you can't associate an object to each distinct odour. It still astonishes me that human noses are so indiscriminate. Even with my eyes closed I could recognise every individual who ventured my way as soon as they entered the room. But there were no creature comforts: no furry mummy-substitute that I could nuzzle and paw; no-one to look after me and bring me back home when I ventured too far away.

In fact, there was nobody to look after me... except Lucy.

Lucy was a miniature human. The floor didn't tremble when she walked by. Her body was soft and I enjoyed plunging my fragile claws into her skin until I smelled fresh blood. Then she'd scream and jump up. There were times when I had to perform midair acrobatics in order to land safely on my feet. She was the nearest thing I had to a mother and when she was cold, she wore adorable woollen jumpers. I could snuggle up and claw them to my heart's content.

When I was hungry, I yowled.

I was greeted with something cold containing an interesting smooth mixture that I lapped up eagerly. Sometimes, it didn't agree with my stomach and there were a few regrettable accidents. I didn't always make it to the strange plastic tray that smelled of the earth. I knew this even though I'd never ventured through the doors into the outside world. Some things are ingrained. Nobody had to tell me to dig a little hole before I did my business. Maybe if I'd still been with my mother, she would have shown me. It's just what you do if you're a cat.

That and licking yourself.

I'd noticed the human habit of frequently scratching, but when I tried with my paws, the result was strangely unsatisfactory. The only way to really relieve an irritating itch is to give it a good lick. Then of course, you get a mouthful of hair which isn't very nice, but I soon discovered that all that entangled hair reappeared when the time was right. I could feel it coming some minutes before, so I made sure I deposited it under a chair where no-one would ever find it.

Lucy was about half the size of the other

two humans who inhabited my closeted world. I just assumed she was still growing. I didn't want to consider the possibility of her staying that size for the rest of her life. That wouldn't be fair. She could hardly reach my food on top of the counter. She seemed to defer on almost everything to the larger specimens, so I assumed they were in charge. There were times when the roles were reversed and Lucy was shouting at them, her face bright red. At times like those, I made myself scarce, hiding behind the sofa and clawing the fabric in places noone would ever notice. It usually ended with Lucy being sent to her room, so I used to sneak in to comfort her.

It was during those times that I learned to read. I would make myself comfortable on her lap and she would open a book and start reading aloud. I soon got the hang of which letters produced which sounds, quickly scanned the text, and then had to wait patiently while Lucy finished the page. There were occasions when I grew so bored that I sank my claws into her legs just for the fun of it.

Together, we laboriously completed endless children's books. Personally, I found many of the plots predictable and I was expected to suspend my disbelief far too regularly. Lucy however, seemed to enjoy them and never complained about their lack of credibility.

Everything in my life served as merely a prelude to the day I was allowed outside. The previous day, the tall long-haired human, who the male referred to as Jo, had grabbed me and proceeded to paint my feet with a colourless substance that smelled oily. I got my revenge by scratching her neck. I then discovered that, contrary to my expectations, the substance on my feet tasted delicious. It began my lifelong love affair with butter. No butter dish was safe when I was in the house. I'd eat it until I was sick. Delicious!

I can still remember the morning of my first trip into the outside world. It must have been a weekend, because Lucy came with me and wouldn't leave me alone. Everything was new: the colours, the smells and the brightness. It was like a different world: grass under my feet and mud in the flower beds. So much more satisfying to dig than that powdery stuff they provided indoors. I didn't really need to go, but felt the urge to dig a hole. Just to give the impression I wasn't losing my mind, I squatted over it for a few seconds, then filled it up again.

My overriding memory of that morning were the smells: the scents of other creatures. Some of them I recognised as feline, coexisting with others I had yet to identify. It made me feel good that there were other cats in the area, although I'd have to teach them that this was *my* garden. I felt a little apprehensive about the other smells. Did they belong to creatures as adorable as cats, or were there bigger, more aggressive animals in the neighbourhood?

It was three, maybe four days before I met another cat. By this time the humans had stopped following me around the garden, even though I deliberately made them wait when they called me in. It's what cats do. I was walking away from the back door and approaching the corner of the shed, when this trespasser appeared. It was about twice my size and predominantly white in colour. It had splashes of brown and black on its flanks in a perfectly symmetrical pattern. Its brow featured what looked like an exploding firework.

Naturally, I swiped at it with my forepaw, catching it with a stinging blow right on the nose. We both retreated a couple of paces and stared at each other in shock. All the hairs on my back were standing on end. I didn't know I could do that. My tail was all flushed out like the thing they used for cleaning the toilet. My back was arched ready to strike again.

'And who would you be?' the intruder demanded.

'Who would I be?' I responded, quick as a flash. Rhetorical questions are also part of a cat's genetic makeup. 'This is *my* garden!'

We both stood there: I watched as a drop of blood fell from its scratched nose. I could see that it felt it, but chose not to pass comment. '*Your* garden?'

'Yes!' I told it shrilly. 'I live here.'

It took a moment to digest the news. I was getting the impression that it wasn't the smartest feline on the block. 'Since when?' it enquired and suddenly relaxed, sitting down.

'A couple of weeks now.'

'I've not seen you before,' it told me, licking a forepaw and wiping it across its injured nose. 'It's been a while since we've had a good old tabby in the neighbourhood,' she remarked mysteriously.

'What do you mean?'

'That's you,' she told me. 'You're a tabby. Your colouring.'

'Oh, right.'

By now, I'd figured that it wasn't offering any threat, so I calmed down the sticky-up hair thing and walked across to sniff its head. I received a gentle head bump which, in your parlance would be, 'How do you do?' Then it stood up and I made the journey around to the rear for a quick sniff. It's amazing how much information those anal glands convey. I've never understood why humans don't do it. I discovered that my companion was old and relaxed, had a dysfunctional kidney on its left-hand side and slight dyspepsia. Then I found the breath catching in my throat. There was something missing! 'You haven't got a...!' I stammered.

'Ah!' Her long tongue flicked the end of

her nose. She flinched a little. 'I'm the one who can make kittens,' she explained. I must have looked confused, because she added, 'You'll find out when you're a bit older.'

'Wow!' I replied. 'Have you made any kittens?'

'Have I?' She put her nose in the air and sniffed the breeze. 'Diamond's coming,' she told me.

'Who?'

'He lives in those houses at the back. Nice old boy.'

'He's your friend?' I asked.

'Yes. There was a time when he was more than a friend, if you know what I mean.' I didn't, so she explained. 'He was the father of six or seven of my kittens... Probably!'

My head twitched as I heard Diamond's regular footsteps approaching. He was huge: great big shoulders protruded from either side of his head and his slow, slouching walk could have been a result of him being grossly overweight. His size was exacerbated by his long silver hair, which appeared perfectly groomed. The uniformity of his coat was broken only by a white diamond on his forehead.

'Flash, my darling,' he greeted my companion, gently bumping heads but not bothering to take a sniff around the back. 'Who scratched your nose?' She took a look in my direction. 'Would you like me to lick it for you?'

She ignored him. 'Diamond, let me introduce our newest neighbour.' They both pointed their noses at me expectantly.

'They call me Yowl,' I told them.

'Noisy kitten, huh?' Diamond said.

'I used to be,' I admitted.

Diamond sat back and tried unsuccessfully to stifle a yawn.

'Heavy night?' Flash asked innocently.

'Slept like a log,' he replied. 'Maybe a little too much breakfast.'

'Diamond's owners give him the best food,' Flash whispered.

'And lots of it!' Diamond added. He may have been old but there was clearly nothing wrong with his ears.

'I can see that!' I told him.

They both turned to stare at me. 'Being rude to your elders is not considered appropriate behaviour in the feline community,' I was told sternly.

'If I were a few years younger, I'd chase you up a tree!' Diamond reflected, yawning.

I remained silent.

I watched as Flash addressed an itch to her rear flank, her left leg sticking vertically into the air. 'Why is your hair so long?' I asked Diamond enviously.

'Ah!' he replied. 'I'm a Persian.'

I took a sharp breath. 'You come all the way from Persia?'

'No. I come all the way from Purley.'

'Where's that?'

'Not very far, really.'

Having completed her grooming, Flash enquired, 'Have you seen Dipper recently?'

Diamond considered the question for some time before responding, 'I haven't seen him for days.'

'That's odd.'

'Who's Dipper?' I asked, just to remind them that I was present.

'Dipper's a homeless cat,' Flash explained. 'He comes round most days. Diamond makes sure he gets enough food.'

'Oh,' I replied.

'Maybe a car got him,' Diamond suggested. They both lowered their heads for a moment's reflection. Maybe they were replaying Dipper's finest moments in their minds. Diamond yawned again. 'I think I'll go and see Cotton. I can have a little sleep in her shed.'

'Alright Stud,' Flash replied. 'See you later.'

He wandered off in the direction of the fence. I watched as he took a lingering look at the top, before briefly shaking his head and squeezing through a hole underneath.

'It wasn't long ago he was leaping over the top,' Flash informed me.

'He probably weighed a little less.'

She shook her head. 'He *has* let himself go recently. He used to be the main man round here.'

I felt something land on my back. I leapt round, twisting my body like a rubber band, ready for anything. There was nothing there! Then it was on my right shoulder. I swung around again, my claws primed. Suddenly there was noise everywhere, like tiny footsteps in the grass.

'It's only rain,' Flash told me solemnly.

'Huh?' I managed as I pirouetted round gracefully, before pushing off and sheltering under Flash's upper body.

'It's rain!' she repeated. 'Water from the sky. It won't hurt you.'

I snuggled up closer to her. 'I don't like it.'

'Neither do I. Let's go home.' And so saying, she turned and departed, leaving me exposed.

I raced back to the kitchen and squeezed through the cat flap. It had been a good morning. I'd met some of the neighbours and they seemed very nice. They didn't appear to pose any great threat. I jumped up onto the windowsill, pressed my nose against the glass and watched the rain falling.

The miserable weather continued all day and late into the evening. I didn't want that rain stuff on my immaculately groomed coat. I got so desperate I had to use the litter tray, which was now only there for emergencies.

2

Dipper's Fate

The following morning dawned grey and misty, but at least it wasn't raining. I skipped out quickly then returned to watch the family prepare for the day ahead. I'd learned that Lucy was in second grade and she had to wear a smart uniform. I'd also managed to identify the adult male as Brian. Although he offered me no hostility, he was uneasy when I sat on him. I didn't mind because his lap was far less comfortable than Jo's. He had bony legs and I found it difficult to settle. It was like sleeping on a bag of spanners.

They didn't forget me. I was given a bowl of crunchy biscuits in the shape of oval animals with a strange triangular tail. The box called them fish. They tasted delicious but they sometimes hurt my teeth.

Eventually, they all departed and I returned to my favourite position on the windowsill overlooking the garden. There was a radiator immediately below, which kept me as warm as toast until it switched itself off. I rarely used my basket to sleep. It had begun to smell and there were a few tiny creatures that could jump prodigious distances. I enjoyed watching them but they tried to sneak into my fur and they made me itch.

I was dozing, happily dreaming of innocent birds on the lawn pecking for worms. I crept up silently behind them and pounced. The thought of their warm blood on my tongue made me purr in excitement. Of course, I hadn't managed to catch one yet. I was still honing my hunting skills. I flicked open an eyelid and watched an extraordinary creature in the garden. It looked a bit like a large grey mouse, but it had a huge bushy tail. I'd chased one earlier, but he'd made his escape by running up the trunk of a tree. I tried to follow, but soon fell down. He'd sat on a branch and laughed at me.

Then I spotted a feline intruder zipping surreptitiously across the grass and into the bushes. It was an unusual colour: pale beige.

I stretched quickly and jumped down to the floor. I may have been young but I had to defend my territory. It might have been a man cat and he might be making unpleasant smells. I wasn't about to let that happen.

I leapt lithely through the cat flap, barely noticing the nasty bump the door gave my back as it swung shut. I'd caught my tail in it the day before. I wouldn't do that again! I needed more practice.

There was something in the air: an unfamiliar smell. My fur rose automatically in response. I crept across the lawn to the bushy area where I'd seen the intruder disappear. I slithered closer and let loose a deafening yowl.

'Yo!' I heard in response. There was a rustling. Then a smiling face appeared between the foliage. He held up a paw to me and said, 'Word up!'

'What?'

'Word up!' He looked at his raised paw. 'Paw bump? Don't leave me hanging.'

He had a very strange accent that I was having difficulty understanding. 'What are you talking about?'

'Newbie!' he spluttered, lowering his paw

to the ground. 'You must be Yowl.'

'I am,' I told him. 'Who are you?'

'You can call me Cool Cat,' he replied. 'I spin the discs; I'm down with the kids; I'm street! Word up?'

I stared at him, wondering what was wrong with him. I'd learned about foreign languages from Lucy's *Countries of the World* book, but the words he used appeared to be my language. It was just the order in which he was employing them that baffled me. Fortunately, just then, I sniffed a familiar smell: Flash. Maybe she could translate for me. 'Morning Flash,' I said in greeting.

She yawned noisily before responding. There was a dark red scab on the end of her nose. 'Morning. I just woke up. Did I miss anything?'

I nodded in Cool Cat's direction.

'Ginger!' she cried. 'I haven't seen you for ages.'

'Ginger?' I enquired.

'Call me Cool Cat. I'm street...' His speech was abruptly interrupted by a smart smack on the cheek from Flash. No claws, you understand, just a tap to get his attention. 'Aw...'

'This is Ginger,' Flash informed me. She turned her attention to him. 'If your mother could see you now!'

Ginger looked suitably chastened. 'My mother...' he wailed. He seemed to have lost his extraordinary accent.

Nobody was in a hurry to enlighten me, so I asked, 'What happened to your mother?'

There was a long silence. 'Nobody knows,' Flash told me. 'All we ever found were... pieces.'

'That's all I had to say goodbye!' Ginger cried, his eyes looking watery. 'I had to bury a tail! That's all there was.'

I gulped. 'What happened?'

They looked at each other conspiratorially. 'Nobody knows...' Ginger started.

'... but it's happened before,' Flash finished.

They both seemed reluctant to tell me more, so I demanded, 'What?'

Flash shook her head sadly. 'You're too young for this. You should still be playing with ping pong balls.'

'Hmm, ping pong balls!' Ginger remarked longingly. 'You should tell him. He needs to know.'

Flash considered for a while before deciding. 'You shouldn't go out at nights,' she told me sternly. 'Someone's killing cats.'

'Why?'

'Nobody knows.'

'That's horrible!' I yowled.

They both nodded.

'Who would do that?'

Flash shrugged.

Just then, I recognised another familiar scent, just before I heard soft rapid steps approaching. 'Nip, nip!' I heard as a manically twitching nose joined the gathering. His bushy tail was erect and taller than his body. 'Nip.'

It was the animal who could run up the side of trees.

'Hello, Secret,' Flash greeted the newcomer.

He couldn't stand still. His whole body darted one way, then another. His nose was constantly twitching and his front claws scratching at the grass. 'Nip.'

'What's it saying?' I asked.

'He said hello,' Flash replied.

'You speak its language?'

Flash looked confused. 'It's your language too,' she explained. 'He just talks incredibly fast and in a very squeaky voice.'

'Nip!'

'Perhaps you could slow down a bit for our new friend, Yowl,' Flash suggested.

'Youchasedmeupatree!' he squeaked with a rapidity that took my brain some seconds to interpret.

'It's what cats do,' I told him.

He giggled shrilly. 'You'llnevercatchme!'

'We'll see about that.' He was returning to his previous racing speech pattern, but now I knew what to listen for, I could understand, just about.

'I found something this morning,' he told us.

Nobody appeared inclined to respond. Flash was busy licking her hind leg and Ginger yawned loudly and lay on the floor.

'I found something this morning,' he repeated.

I only replied because I thought ignoring him was rude. 'What?'

'An ear!'

Flash had moved on to scratching herself under her right leg. She gave a shake and sat down again. 'Whose ear?'

'Don't know.'

She didn't appear concerned. She stretched out on a sunny patch of grass and mumbled, 'Must be time for a little nap.'

'It was a cat's ear!' Secret whispered.

'A cat's ear?' came a deep voice. The wind must have been in the wrong direction. I hadn't detected anyone approaching. 'What's this about a cat's ear?' Diamond made his leisurely way towards us, sat, and broke wind loudly.

'Manners!' cried Flash, who was lying uncomfortably close.

'Pardon!' he mumbled in apology. 'Tell me about the ear,' he asked Secret.

'It's black.'

Diamond's head dropped marginally. 'Show me.' I think he already knew what he was going to find.

Secret turned and scampered away. Within a few seconds, he was a mere grey blob disappearing into the distance. We reached the end of the garden and stopped. We had no idea where he'd gone. 'Secret!' Diamond bellowed.

About ten seconds later, his head appeared above the wooden fence. 'What?'

'Slow down!' he was told. 'We're trying to follow.'

'If you'd lose some weight, you might be a bit quicker,' Secret pointed out. 'This way.'

Slowly, Diamond wandered beside the fence until he reached a broken plank. Even so, it was a tight squeeze negotiating his great bulk through. I took a look at the top of the fence. I thought I could do it. It was a big moment for me. I'd never left the relative safety of my garden before. I had no idea what to expect. I took a run at it, leaping gracefully and using my fragile claws to gain purchase. It wasn't easy, but eventually I balanced on the top, panting. I was only three months old, remember? I was startled as Ginger almost soundlessly arrived next to me. 'Word up?' I suggested.

He purred in response. Then, without waiting for me, he flew down the fence and landed comfortably in a flowerbed. I watched in envy. I was hugely pleased with myself for managing to climb to the top. Now it looked very high. I was scared. 'Ginger!' I cried.

'What?'

'How do I get down?'

He turned back to me. 'Just lead down with your front paws as far as you can go, then jump and land on your feet.'

He made it sound easy and, having watched him, he made it look easy too. I took a deep breath and stretched down as far as I could reach with my front legs. They were only half as long as his. When I was fully extended, I jumped. My front legs buckled on impact and my chin hit the soft earth with a thud. My body rolled over and I ended up lying in the mud. I picked myself up groggily.

Ginger had been watching my attempts. 'There you go. Nothing to it!' he remarked and turned away.

The impact had slammed my jaws shut, with the result that I bit my tongue painfully. I could taste blood. Dejectedly, I wandered after him. I couldn't afford to lose them. I didn't know the way.

Further along, we encountered Flash and Diamond sitting closely together like the old married couple I'd seen in Lucy's *My Family* book. 'He's gone again,' Diamond informed us.

I was too concerned nursing my stinging tongue to notice the time, but it was some minutes before Secret returned. 'Sorry, I found an acorn. I had to hide it for winter.'

'How did you hide it?' I asked.

He looked at me as if I was stupid. 'I dug a hole and buried it. Now, it's this way,' he told us springing away once more.

I didn't move. 'How will you find it again?'

Everyone stopped and turned to look at me. 'I'm a squirrel,' he told me, as if that explained everything.

'Right.' I trudged along after them.

We passed several houses, negotiating a couple of dilapidated fences. Then Diamond started to pant. 'Not as young as I used to be,' he wheezed.

Flash turned and stood next to him with concern showing on her face. 'How are you feeling, Stud?'

'Oh,' he sighed. 'Just need a short...' Suddenly, he pointed his nose towards the fence. 'You remember Bully?'

Flash frowned and turned to look in the

direction he indicated. 'Of course!' she exclaimed. 'It was here!' She turned back to Diamond and together, they started to laugh.

'Boy, that dog was stupid!' he managed between chuckles.

'He never learnt.'

They continued to chuckle together, remembering old times. 'Who was Bully?' I asked.

They took a moment to compose themselves. Then Flash started, 'He was a big brute of a bulldog. Used to live in that garden.'

Diamond took up the story. 'Every evening, me and Flash would come round at feeding time.'

'And it was good food!' Flash interjected.

'Oh, yes. No canned food for Bully. Anyway, he'd start to eat and one of us would race down the garden and jump on top of his kennel. Sometimes, he didn't even hear us. We had to let him know we were there. When we'd got his attention, we jumped off and raced back up the garden and sat on the fence. He chased after us...'

'The noise he used to make!'

'And he just jumped up at the fence, barking.'

'Meanwhile,' Flash prompted.

'Meanwhile, the other one of us used to sneak down and finish his dinner.'

'It was good!' Flash remembered.

'Real meat. No rubbish,' he agreed. 'When we'd finished, we used to watch him go back to his bowl.'

'He'd spend ages looking around, wondering who'd eaten it.'

They both collapsed in another fit of giggles. 'Ah, well,' Diamond went on. 'I always swore I wouldn't be like those old cats who kept telling me everything was better in their day.'

Flash nodded in agreement. 'You remember your aunt Spot?' she asked.

'Oh, yes. She was right, wasn't she?'

I looked up enquiringly and Flash explained. 'She used to tell us that getting old was a trial. Nothing worked as well as it used to.'

'She told us to enjoy every moment while we were young, because too soon, it would be too late.'

They paused for a moment remembering absent friends. 'We didn't have a bad life, did we?' Flash asked.

Diamond nodded slowly. 'And it's not finished yet,' he pointed out. 'Let's go. Anyone see that squirrel?'

'Secret!' Ginger yelped.

Tiny footsteps approached. We all looked around but couldn't see anything. 'Nip!' There he was, right above us, hanging upside down from a branch. 'I thought I saw a cob nut,' he told us.

'Lead on,' Diamond instructed, dragging himself back to his feet. Secret leapt straight to the floor and took off again. We followed. I noticed that Flash never ventured too far from Diamond's side.

Secret led us down a footpath between houses until we were standing on a pavement, close to the edge of a road. There were no pedestrians and no cars. 'Quiet,' Secret remarked. 'It's over by the red tower,' he told us.

I looked around for a red tower. 'You mean the pillar box?'

'What's a pillar box?' he asked bemused.

'It's that red thing over there,' I replied.

They all turned to look at me. 'How do you know that?' Ginger asked.

'I read it in a book.'

They continued to stare. Several mouths had dropped open. 'You can read?' Flash asked.

'Of course,' I replied.

Ginger shook his head vigorously. 'No! Cats can't read!'

'Why not?' I asked.

He stood there with his mouth open. 'They just can't!'

Secret looked as though he didn't believe a word of it, but led the way to the pavement edge. I lifted my leg to take the next step.

'Stop!' Flash screamed. I stood motionless, waiting, my leg hanging in the air. 'Sit down!' she ordered. She then proceeded to give me a three minute lecture on the danger of roads. 'Do you know how many cousins we've lost to cars?' she screamed. I shook my head. I didn't know she had any cousins. 'You might be able to read but you have to learn how to cross the road!'

When she'd finished, we all looked right, left, and right again. We used our sensitive ears to listen for any oncoming traffic. Finally, we were allowed to scamper across, with the exception of Diamond who crossed at his own leisurely pace.

'It's round here,' Secret told us scuttling around in a pile of leaves. He used his front paws to clear a patch until he'd exposed what he was looking for. 'There!'

Diamond made his way over, dragging Flash in his wake. He bent to take a closer look and sniffed carefully. 'Dipper,' he remarked.

Flash double checked his findings and confirmed with a sharp nod. 'Dipper.'

Ginger and I went to have a look. There really wasn't much to see. Secret had managed to identify by scent, what could easily have been another leaf or piece of rubbish. It was small, curled and black. The edge was very straight and unnatural. It didn't look like it had been torn with claws or bitten by teeth.

Just then, we heard footsteps coming down the alley. We ducked furtively under a bush in a neighbouring garden until they'd passed. A white mini sped up the road making an unusual whining sound. We sat solemnly until everything was quiet again.

'Tell me about Dipper,' I suggested.

Diamond shook his head. 'He came from up north, somewhere by the sea. He got caught in the back of a van, sleeping. He couldn't get out. When the van stopped, he was here.' He looked at Flash.

'He was nice enough. Spoke with a funny accent.'

'He never had a home here,' Diamond went on. 'He just made the best of what he had. Never complained. We helped when we could...'

'Maybe...' I started. 'Maybe he's...' I was thinking along the lines of a cat losing an ear doesn't necessarily have to be fatal. Maybe he was still around, but not hearing anyone call.

Diamond shook his head wearily. 'No,' he stated emphatically. 'There's more.' He put his nose in the air and sniffed theatrically. Then he turned his head towards the alleyway. 'Over here.'

We followed him, our undisputed leader.

His nose would lead us in the right direction. He started to dig in a pile of leaves, similar to Secret before. I could smell an unpleasant odour. He sat back on the cold floor and waited while we all filed past. I didn't know Dipper. I'd never had the chance to meet him but he was definitely dead. He had no family to mourn him, but both Flash and Diamond would ensure his passing didn't go unnoticed.

'It's just like my mother,' Ginger whispered.

Flash and Diamond looked at each other, before nodding.

'No-one is safe,' Diamond told us.

*

We made our way home by a slightly easier route. We were all conscious that Diamond wasn't capable of anything energetic, let alone climbing fences. We said our goodbyes to Secret, not forgetting to thank him, and made our way back to my house. Diamond was silent throughout, lost in thought. Flash tried to make conversation a couple of times, but soon realised it was hopeless.

When we reconvened in my back garden, Diamond was still brooding. 'I wonder...' he mused aloud.

'What is it, Stud?' Flash enquired eagerly.

He looked up at the treetops. 'Hewt,' he suggested. 'He sees everything at night.'

She looked at him sadly. 'I think that ship has sailed, Diamond.'

I'd lost track of the conversation. I didn't know who Hewt was and I didn't know which ship had sailed where. I looked at Ginger for assistance.

'He's an old owl,' he told me. 'Lives in that tree over there.'

'Which ship did he sail?'

He shook his head impatiently. 'It's a saying. Hewt used to be a friend. Now...'

'What happened?'

'It was before I was born,' he told me.

Flash sauntered over to continue. 'He lost his partner. She was... special. He blamed cats.'

'Why?'

'He searched for her for days. Never slept. He eventually found her body over on the fields. It had been... torn apart.'

'That doesn't sound like a cat,' Ginger suggested.

Flash nodded. 'More like a fox, we thought.'

'So, why...?'

She took a deep breath. 'She had cat hairs in her talons; there were cat's footprints around the body; and the area smelled of cats.'

'You were there?' I asked.

She nodded. 'Diamond and I were out looking for her too. We heard Hewt's screams from miles away. We came over and... the body! It was so sad.' She looked on the point of tears. 'She was very... special.' She walked away and lay down next to Diamond.

'In all your life,' Diamond went on, 'you'll meet a few animals who'll really make a mark on you. Change your life. For the better! Princess was one of them. She made everything seem... better.'

'But Hewt...' I started.

Diamond lay his head on his front legs. 'After that, Hewt didn't want to be around anyone anymore. He just gave up. Stays all day in his nest, hunts at night, just enough to keep himself alive, sleeps the rest of the time. He doesn't want to know.'

'Oh, we tried!' Flash insisted, when she saw my look of confusion. 'Every day, we took him a mouse. Every day, we pleaded with him to let us help him. But...' She shook her head. 'He never came down.'

'A loss like that is difficult to bear,' Diamond added, staring wistfully into the treetops. 'Animals like that only come around once in a lifetime.'

A human was making a shrill noise trying to attract someone's attention. Ginger sighed. 'Sounds like it's time to go,' he mumbled and wandered off.

I spent the rest of the afternoon thinking about Hewt and the perfect life he'd been denied by some rogue animal.

*

In some respects, cats are the opposite of humans. We liked to get a full sixteen hours sleep a day. I was young, so I still required a little more. The evenings were always good for an hour or two curled up on Lucy's lap or on her bed. My humans had started to feed me a different kind of food, one for adult cats, it said on the packet. It was very nice, but it contained large chunks that I sometimes had difficulty chewing, and it gave me terrible wind. I don't think the humans noticed because, as I've explained, their sense of smell is rubbish.

That night, we went to bed as usual. I was allowed to stay with Lucy until she had to put the lights out. She opened a new book and we began to start reading. It was by a writer named Enid Blyton, *The Secret Seven*. I read with interest, as usual, impatiently waiting for Lucy to finish each page. She read very slowly. After struggling through five pages in half an hour, we were joined by her mother who proceeded to read aloud. That was better! The story raced along at a good pace, but just when it was getting interesting, we were told it was time to turn out the light. Disappointed, I wandered downstairs to the kitchen. I took a look in my bowl: empty. I curled up on the windowsill and went to sleep.

3

Ally and Patch – Dogs!

The next morning, the sun was shining. I pushed through the cat flap and tiptoed up the still dewy lawn. I basked in the sun's rays. It had been too long since it had shone. I'd read in Lucy's *Healthy Children* book that sunshine was essential for our vitamin D requirements. I feared that living in this place could result in a permanent deficiency, especially since I wasn't keen on the green vegetables that also provided it. The book included a chapter on people called vegetarians. I'm a carnivore. I struggled to understand the concept.

Ginger raced down the garden, leaping in the air and twisting his body. He looked like a young kitten. I briefly wondered why I didn't have the urge to do the same.

'Yo, Yowl! How's it hanging?' As usual, I had no idea what he was talking about. 'Feel the warmth, man!'

I think he was enjoying the sun too.

'Nip!'

I looked this way and that, but I couldn't see Secret. Cats have extremely well-developed senses: smell, sight and hearing, but I still had no idea where he was. Finally, he scampered down the trunk of an old apple tree and joined us in the sun. He scurried around, describing a circle with us in the middle. 'Nutter told me something yesterday,' he started.

'Who's that?' I felt prompted to ask.

'She's my partner. She's looking after our kits,' he explained.

'Oh! Don't you help?'

'I take them food,' he told us defensively.

'How many are there?'

'Five. She has to feed them every few hours.'

'That must be tough,' I suggested.

'It's tough finding enough food. I'm worn out,' he proceeded to yawn in a highly theatrical way.

'Well, what did she say?' I reminded him.

'She saw a strange man in the middle of the night.'

I looked at Ginger.

'What was strange about him, bro?' he asked.

'He was tall and he was carrying something shiny. She thought it might be a knife.'

We both looked up sharply. 'A tall man!' Ginger cried. As descriptions went, it didn't narrow the field significantly, but it was a start.

'When was this?' I asked.

He glanced around uncertainly. 'Weeks ago?'' he queried. 'Before we had the kits.'

'Where?' I asked.

'On the footpath near the school.'

I didn't know the footpath but Ginger nodded wisely. 'What happened?' he went on.

'A car drove past and he put the thing in his jacket.' It was a bit of an anticlimactic story. 'Odd thing...' he continued.

'Yes?' we urged.

'He smelled of food,' he added gravely.

'What sort of food?' I asked.

'Cat food. She could smell it even though she wasn't close to him.'

'So that's how he does it,' Ginger mused.

'What did he look like?' I probed.

'She said he was... human, and tall.'

'Could she be a little more specific?' I asked hopefully.

'I don't know. They all look human...' he replied. 'Oh, yes! He had a hat.'

'What sort of hat?'

'A black woolly hat pulled down over his ears.'

'Hmm,' I pondered. 'Interesting.' The weather was cold. The leaves were falling. It wasn't exactly surprising that someone out in the middle of the night would choose to wear a woolly hat. 'What kind of jacket?' I asked.

'Ah, yes... Jacket. I umm...' He thought for a moment. 'I didn't ask.'

'Can you find out what she remembers?' Ginger requested.

'Yes, but right now, I have to find food for the little ones.'

'What do they eat?' I asked.

'Nuts, out of their shells, of course. And anything soft, apples, grapes...'

'We've got some grapes in the kitchen. Want some?'

'That'd be great,' he replied.

I dashed off to the kitchen and lithely leapt up onto the counter next to the fruit bowl. I experienced a little difficulty detaching a small branch from the bigger bunch. In the end, I resorted to gnawing through. I departed for the garden carrying a bunch of six grapes in my teeth. They were surprisingly heavy.

'Oh, wow!' he shrieked in an even higher pitched voice than normal. 'Now I won't have to forage today.'

'In return for Nutter's help identifying this human,' I told him laying them on the grass.

'I'll find out everything she knows,' he told us scuttling away with the stem held firmly in his teeth.

Suddenly, there was wind, violent wind, blowing downwards on my head and ruffling my immaculate fur coat. I turned quickly and therefore missed the landing of a fat pigeon inches ahead of me.

'Digger!' Ginger cried enthusiastically.

'Morning all,' he replied. 'Who's this now?' I was still trying to rearrange my beautiful coat after the abrupt gust, feverishly licking it down into place. 'Sorry,' he told me. 'Couldn't resist.'

I pounced in his direction, confidently expecting my claws to dig through the feathers and embed themselves in his tender flesh. He took a casual hop backwards, looking bored.

'Aren't we supposed to chase you?' I asked.

He looked me up and down. 'I'm bigger than you.'

'Nothing a bit more exercise wouldn't cure,' I mumbled. I was surprised he could still fly.

'This is Yowl,' Ginger informed him. 'He's young.'

'Wait!' I cried. 'You fly in the sky, right?'

'Err, yes,' he replied. 'That's the idea.'

'So you see everything?'

'Well, I see quite a lot,' he told me. 'I do have a slight astigmatism in my left eye.'

I looked at him blankly. It meant nothing to me. I needed Lucy to start reading medical books. 'What can you tell us about the cat killer?'

His eyes focused on mine. 'It's true then?'

'Yes, it's true,' Flash responded, smoothly joining the gathering and sitting down. 'No-one is safe outside at night.'

'I did hear some dogs talking...' he started.

'Dogs!' I wailed.

Everyone went quiet. 'I think you need to reconsider the stereotypes already implanted in your brain,' Digger told me solemnly. 'Generally, everyone around here gets along.'

'No chasing?' I asked in surprise.

'You can chase if you want. You're young. The rest of us just want a quiet life.'

'You could always chase mice,' Ginger suggested.

I considered it. 'They're not our friends?'

'Well, there was that one...' Ginger began. 'What was she called?'

'Twitcher,' Flash supplied.

'She was fun,' he went on. 'You remember when she used to play with the electricity in her house? The humans thought they had ghosts!' They both descended into fits of laughter. It was some time before they noticed the confused expression on my face. 'She used to nibble the cables under the floorboards and expose the wires,' he explained. 'Then she pushed them together with a stick. All the lights went off.' They continued their giggling.

'Isn't that dangerous?' I asked.

'Very!' Flash replied. 'She stopped after she burned her right hand.'

They were sombre for some moments before Ginger continued, 'What do you call a judge with no thumbs?' he asked me.

'I don't know,' I replied, shaking my head.

'Justice fingers!' he told me and they descended into laughter again. Even Digger joined in.

'The old ones are always the best,' Ginger wheezed through his laughter.

I decided to try a joke I'd read in one of Lucy's books. 'What do you call a blind deer?'

'I don't know that one,' Ginger responded. 'What?'

'No idea,' I told him.

It took a few seconds, but eventually, they both chuckled.

Digger decided to join in the frivolities. 'I once knew a fairy called Nuff,' he told us.

'Fairy Nuff!' Ginger responded immediately.

Once the laughter had died down, Flash passed a forearm across her eyes and asked, 'What did you say about dogs?'

Digger was busy investigating something in the grass. His name was evidently well-earned. He took a break. 'Oh, yes! I heard Ally talking with Patch. They were saying someone was after cats.'

'When was this?' Flash asked.

He looked a little ruffled. 'In the past,' he told us. 'I used the past tense.'

'How many days in the past,' Flash probed.

He thought, his eyes tightly closed. 'Several?'

'Pigeons are well known for their total lack of time awareness,' a gruff voice told us.

'Morning Stud!' Flash greeted Diamond.

'When every day is the same,' he continued, 'there is nothing to gauge the passing of time.'

We quickly brought him up to date with developments: Nutter's strange man with what might be a knife and Digger overhearing the dogs' conversation.

'Eavesdropping again?' Diamond suggested.

'I just happened to overhear...'

'Pigeons are the biggest gossips in the animal world,' Diamond told us. 'You should always be careful what you say when they're around.'

'That's a bit strong!' Digger cried.

'They have no social conscience, you see.' Digger looked sullen but didn't challenge the statement. 'So,' Diamond went on, 'let's go and have a talk with Ally.'

'A dog!' I gasped.

'Yes,' he replied calmly. 'Nice old boy. He's my neighbour, you know.'

'Doesn't he chase you?'

He scoffed. 'He did when he was young. Never caught me though.' He stretched his forearms in front of him. It was clear he couldn't quite make it to the ground. Old age, I supposed.

He sauntered off the way he'd come with everyone following except Digger, who took to the sky. I lingered some way behind the others, not relishing the thought of our upcoming appointment with a dog. Some of them were huge and had very sharp teeth. I hadn't forgotten the story of 'Little Red Riding Hood', although that was a wolf and there had been someone there to save her.

We followed the same path as the previous day and I'm happy to report that my fence dismount was much improved. Ginger gave me an appreciative nod. 'Learning!' he remarked.

We passed another two gardens, Diamond always taking the path of least resistance. Finally, he squeezed under a chicken wire fence and boldly walked down the garden towards a large wooden kennel. 'Ally!' he called as he approached. Presumably, unannounced visitors were greeted with a hostile reception.

'Woof!' came the response.

I hung back, trying to conceal myself behind Flash's bulky torso.

'How are you, old boy?' Diamond asked unnecessarily loudly.

Awoken from his slumber, Ally appeared around the corner of his kennel – beige and white with a big black nose: an Alsatian. He stretched and drew himself to his full height. He was massive. He towered over the unconcerned Diamond, who busied himself attending to an itch around his... hind quarters.

'Diamond! Haven't seen you in days.'

'Well, I'm not as young as I used to be,' he responded sadly.

'Tell me about it,' he agreed. "Who's this?' he remarked with a loud bark, springing at me with alarming malice. I was halfway up the nearest tree by the time I looked around. They were all laughing at me. 'Come on down, Junior,' Ally told me. 'Just joking.'

I could feel the tension leaving my body. All my hair was flattening. It just left me with one problem. 'Ginger!' I called.

He strolled over slowly. 'Yes.'

'How do I get down?' I was clinging to the tree trunk as tightly as I could and my little claws were beginning to ache.

'Well, it's simple. You sort of turn around and run down,' he explained. I tried my best, but once again I found myself banging my chin against the ground when my front legs buckled. 'Or... Like that!' he remarked as I picked myself off the ground.

Diamond made the introductions and I stood very still as Ally came across for a quick sniff. I stood my ground. I didn't want him to know that I was terrified.

'Good to meet you, kid.'

I just nodded in return. I was already on high alert, so when I caught a languid movement out of the corner of my eye, I stopped dead. 'What's that?' I cried. It was a bizarre animal. It looked like a squashed green coconut with a head and four legs poking out.

'It's a tortoise,' Diamond explained.

I took a step closer. 'What does it do?'

'Um...' he started. 'Um...' he continued. 'What does it do?' he repeated. 'Nothing, really. It just walks around very, very, slowly, eating the grass.'

I looked at it, confused. It stared back at me, chewing.

'He's quite friendly,' Diamond told me. 'Take a closer look.'

I approached with caution. The tortoise didn't move, just continued its unhurried chewing. I glanced enquiringly at Diamond.

'See?' he asked, nodding at the creature.

I looked back. It had gone! 'Where did he go?' I cried.

Diamond chuckled. 'He's hiding inside his shell.'

'Why?'

'He thinks you're a danger to him.'

'Can I eat him?'

'No!'

'Then I'm not a danger.'

'No, but *he* doesn't know that,' he explained.

'Extraordinary creature!' I exclaimed dismissively.

'Hey!' I heard the long drawn out single syllable in an unusually deep voice. 'Tortoises have feelings too, you know!'

I shook my head and turned back to join Diamond and Flash. I couldn't understand humans. Why would they indulge themselves with a creature that clearly wasn't capable of returning any affection? Why didn't they stick to loyal and lovable cats?

Diamond wasted no time getting down to business, asking Ally about his conversation with Patch about the cat killer.

'How did you hear about that?' he asked in surprise.

Then the wind was back, blowing hard; a fluttering of wings followed by a long 'Coo'.

'Sorry,' came a breathless voice. 'Went to the wrong garden.'

'Ah! Say no more.' Ally turned his head towards me. 'Never tell a pigeon anything you don't want everyone to know,' he advised.

I nodded in agreement. I didn't want to upset him.

'It was Patch,' he told us. 'He saw someone suspicious. Then he came across a tail.'

'Wah!' screamed Ginger. It was all too close to the story of his mother.

'Where's Patch?' Flash asked.

'Asleep, I expect.'

'Indoors?'

Ally nodded. 'He hasn't been feeling well for days.'

'What's the problem?'

'I think it's his heart,' he told us miserably. 'I don't think he has long left.'

Everyone's head dropped for a few seconds, except mine. I could understand the solemn ritual for a dead animal, but Patch was still alive. 'Can we talk to him?' I asked.

'I'll see if he's awake.' He walked away in the direction of the house. If I had to choose a new word to use, it would be lugubrious, that about summed him up.

Flash turned to me. 'They were real trouble in the old days, Ally and Patch. Nothing was safe. Ally used to jump up and pull all the neighbours' washing off their lines.'

'And Patch was always digging holes in their lawns,' Diamond explained.

'And burying... things,' Flash added mysteriously.

'They turned out to be real Gents, the pair of them.'

'You remember that time they saved a baby from falling in the canal?'

'Oh, yes! Stopped the pram right on the edge,' Diamond remembered smiling. 'And they caught that burglar in the street.'

'That's right! Wouldn't let him go until the police turned up.'

'He still had the stolen goods on him.'

Ally reappeared with another dog of indeterminate lineage. He was about a third of Ally's height and it was clear where the name Patch came from. He looked like a raggedy doll sewn together from cloth patches. 'Someone looking for me?' he asked in the deepest voice I'd ever heard.

Flash looked concerned. 'How are you, Patch?'

He sat down carefully. 'Feeling a bit... you know, chesty. Breathing's a bit difficult.'

'Can't they take you to a vet?'

'Did that,' he replied. 'There's something wrong with my heart. They can't fix it.'

'I'm sorry,' she responded with a sympathetic smile.

'I've had a good run,' he assured us. 'My good luck to have been paired with Ally.' He looked at his friend in appreciation. 'You lot haven't been all bad either. I've been lucky to know you all.' That prompted another heads down moment of reflection. 'Who's the new boy?'

'That's Yowl,' Ginger told him.

He nodded in my direction. 'Good to meet you, Yowl. You stick with this lot, you won't go far wrong.'

'I will,' I replied, although I was already concerned about Diamond. He was getting slower every day.

'So, how can I help you?' Patch enquired.

'You know something about the cat killer?' Flash prompted.

'Oh!' He sounded surprised. 'The Tall Man? He still going? I bit him once.'

'You did?' I asked.

He nodded gravely, taking several deep rasping breaths. 'I thought he was alright to begin with. He'd put some food on the ground for a cat. I was feeling a bit peckish myself, so I wandered over. I thought he was trying to help.' He came to an abrupt halt, breathing heavily.

'What happened?' Diamond prompted.

'He got this... I thought it was a pen, out of his jacket. It was silver. Looked just like a pen,' he told us. We listened transfixed.

'What did he do?' Flash asked.

'He bent down over the cat, who was still eating. Typical cat!' he scoffed. 'Stomach bigger than its brain.'

'Steady!' Flash admonished.

He looked at her with his pale eyes. 'You know, I always liked you,' he told her.

'I know,' Flash told him.

'So,' I prompted, interrupting their mutual appreciation. 'You thought he was bending down to write a message on this cat with a pen.'

He gave me an impatient look. 'No! He held it up in his fist, like this.' He held up his front paw. It was obvious he was adopting a stabbing posture. 'So, I dashed across and bit his hand.'

'Straight!' shouted Ginger. 'Respect!'

Patch looked at Ginger. 'I've never had the slightest idea what you're talking about. Must be a generation thing,' he pondered.

'He's complimenting you,' Flash explained.

'Oh! Okay.' He resumed his story, 'Anyway, the pen... thing fell to the ground and it wasn't a pen at all.'

'What was it?' I asked.

'It had a wicked looking blade on the end, real sharp.'

'That sounds like a scalpel,' Digger suggested.

'What's that?'

'A really sharp knife they use in hospitals.'

'Was it a proper bite?' I asked, wondering

whether we could identify the culprit by a scar.

'Oh, yes! I felt bone on my teeth. There was a lot of blood.'

That was good news. 'What did he do after you bit him?'

'He screamed, the cat scarpered. Tried to kick me, he did, but I was too quick.'

'When was this?' Diamond asked.

He cast his mind back. 'Some time ago, now. Back when the evenings were long and the sun was shining. In the...'

'The summer?' I suggested.

'That's the word I was looking for! Escaped me for a minute.'

'What did he look like?'

'Apart from being tall? He was... human.' He held out his paws in front of him. 'He had... a hand with a bite mark.'

We looked at each other. Our eyewitnesses were turning out to be rather vague. 'Which hand?' I asked.

'His...' He held out his paws in front of him in turn. 'This one!' he cried, holding up his left.

I was seeking definite confirmation. 'He

was holding the knife in his left hand?'

'Yes, this one.' He indicated again.

'But you can't tell us anything about him?'

'He was definitely... No, I can't!' he admitted.

'Nip!' He'd managed to sneak up on us all again, totally undetected. 'Hi, Patch. You alright?'

Patch just stared at him, his expression not changing a jot. 'I used to be able to understand you, sorry.'

Secret took great pains to speak very slowly. 'I said, are you alright?'

'Not really,' he replied. 'I'm dying.'

'No!' he shrieked. 'You can't die. We all love you.'

'My time is coming,' he said with a languid shake of his head. 'But I've greatly enjoyed the time I've spent with you all.'

'Even Digger?' Secret enquired.

'Even Digger. You always know where you stand with a pigeon.'

Digger cooed appreciatively, accepting it as a compliment. I wasn't certain it was meant that way.

We all thanked Patch, wished him well by gently bumping noses, and allowed him to return to his warm bed. We reconvened in Diamond's garden to discuss our findings. I couldn't concentrate. Something smelled delicious. I was distractedly looking around for the source.

'... Yowl?' I looked up in surprise. Someone had mentioned my name, asked me a question. I hadn't been listening.

'Pardon?'

With a sigh, Diamond wandered towards the house and grabbed a plastic dish in his teeth. 'Here you go, Junior.' He dropped it at my feet.

'Wow!' I sniffed eagerly. 'What is this? It smells like ambrosia.'

'What's that?' he asked.

I tried unsuccessfully to tell him with my mouth full. I swallowed hastily and then told him, 'The food of the gods.'

'Really?' He looked surprised. 'Well, this is called salmon,' he told me.

I scoffed it down greedily, everyone watching me. 'Miss your breakfast this morning?'

Flash asked.

'No,' I replied with my mouth full again. I stood very still. Everyone was staring at me. I decided it was time to display a little maturity. It broke my heart, but I left a little in the bowl and proceeded to clean myself.

'Did you hear what Secret said?' Flash asked.

'No!' I admitted. 'I was... distracted.'

She sighed heavily. 'Tell him, Secret.'

'It's like this...' he started. 'Nutter thinks she recognised the man with the knife.'

'The Tall Man? Really!' I cried. 'Who was it?'

'She can't remember.'

'Oh,' I responded, disappointed. 'But squirrels' memories are really good!' I reminded him. 'How else would you remember where you buried all your nuts?'

'Well, to be perfectly honest, I don't remember where I bury *all* of them,' he admitted. 'She said he was tall too, and she knows she's seen him before.'

'Doing what?'

'That's just it. She can't remember, but

she's definitely seen him before.'

I sat back, having finished my brief after-food clean-up. 'Can't she get out and have a look around?' I suggested.

He shrieked loudly. 'Who'll look after our kits?'

'Err, you?'

He shrieked again: a real ear piercing shriek. 'I don't know the first thing about kits!'

'Maybe it's time you learned,' Flash suggested, although I didn't suppose she'd had a lot of help raising her kittens.

'I'm a forager!' he went on. 'I forage! Nutter looks after the babies.'

Flash turned away, unimpressed.

I tried to stifle a yawn. I'd been up for over an hour. It was time I got some sleep. We all agreed to meet again in the afternoon, but I didn't really think we would. Diamond was old and seldom ventured outside his garden twice in one day. I wandered back home feeling an unsettling mixture of frustration and optimism. I felt we were closing in on the Tall Man, but Nutter would need to provide something by way of identification. I was also thinking about Hewt. If we could enlist his help, I had no doubt we'd find him quickly. Owls have exceedingly good eyesight and he was up and about at exactly the right time: the middle of the night, when the rest of us were sleeping.

I tiptoed inside the house. Everyone was out. Lucy was at school and her mum had a part-time job at a doctor's surgery. She'd be home in time to collect Lucy from school and, more importantly, give me my lunch.

A brief glance through the kitchen doorway confirmed the house was deserted, but I noticed something on the mat inside the front door. Somebody had delivered something through the letter box. I knew it couldn't be the postman: he was unlikely to be around until mid-afternoon. My curiosity was aroused. I wandered over and sat alongside a small, blank piece of card. Why would anyone send us a blank piece of card through the letterbox? I had a leisurely yawn and then came to the conclusion that I was looking at the back. It must say something on the other side. I pushed it and flicked it, dug my claws underneath it and bent it, and finally managed to flip it over.

I was confronted with several pictures of a female tabby cat. She was quite pretty. I started reading at the top. 'Tabitha has been missing since 18th November. She is seven years old and went missing from St John's Road...' I read all the information. Tabitha had a medical condition and had never gone missing before. Her owners were very worried about her. They assumed that she'd been trapped in a shed or garage and couldn't get out. She loved jumping through windows and maybe she'd got herself locked in.

I thought about it. Of course, that was one entirely plausible explanation. I felt there was another. I feared that Tabitha may have become another victim of the Tall Man. I was scared. I didn't think I'd be able to sleep at all. I lay down beside Tabitha's picture and closed my eyes to think.

4

Big Red – The Leader of the Foxes

I must have been more tired than I thought. Several hours later, I was disturbed by the rattle of the letterbox. I had a good yawn and a thorough stretch, followed by a few leftover, hard, fish-shaped biscuits. Their appeal had significantly diminished since my morning encounter with salmon. I rounded it off with a drink of nice, cold water. I was occasionally given a bowl of milk, which was delicious, but when you're thirsty, there's nothing like cold water.

Dutifully, I checked the post, ensuring that nothing threatened the security of the house. Then I retraced my steps and settled on the windowsill. The clouds had returned and the leaves on the trees shimmered in the wind. I wouldn't be surprised to see rain before long. I decided to venture out to relieve myself before it started.

When I returned, suitably refreshed, Lucy and her mother were back. I sensed a problem: Lucy's face was red and she stormed upstairs without even giving me a stroke. Ah, well! I circled her mother's legs with such persistence that she was left with only two options: trip over me or feed me. She sighed as she delved into the food cupboard and retrieved a sachet that wasn't salmon. I was hungry. I ate it anyway. Most of it. I didn't want to appear greedy. I cleaned myself and crept up the stairs. Lucy was sitting at her desk, staring into space. I jumped up and rubbed my nose against her hand. I got a stroke in return, but I could tell her heart wasn't really in it. She mumbled something about homework. 'Homework!' she grumbled. 'I'm only six!' I nodded in agreement. It sounded a little young to be given homework, but then she went on, 'I got a bad mark in my test, so now I have to work.' I purred in sympathy. Having experienced for myself the difficulty she'd had learning to read, I secretly thought some extra lessons would benefit her in the long run. I made a hasty exit to allow her to concentrate.

Halfway down the stairs, the letterbox rattled again and the local paper fell onto the mat. I wasn't having that! I leapt on it and dug in my claws, shredding the edge of the front page. Well, I was only young. Then I jumped on my vanquished foe, looking down in triumph to see the haunted look of defeat. Instead I saw *Croydon Cat Killer: Residents Demand Action.* I took in a sharp breath and read on. Police had received details of the suspicious deaths of over seventy cats. Mrs Emmanuelle Trantor had been interviewed, expressing her disgust at the police's lack of action. *They don't appear to be taking it seriously. If it was babies being murdered, they'd have set up a task force and be flooding the area with policemen.* I'm sure she was right but I didn't understand the comparison. How likely was it that babies would be crawling around the streets on their own in the middle of the night?

Over seventy cats!

The article went on to describe their fate. I felt nauseous. This was definitely the work of a disturbed mind. Mrs Trantor finished her interview by advising, *I believe this to be the work of a single sick individual. He must be apprehended and brought to justice. Everyone must be vigilant.* She was right. We all had a responsibility to help find this man and ensure that he received the punishment he deserved.

I went out, squeezed under the fence and yowled outside Flash's back door. She poked her head out, appearing reluctant to venture further. 'It's raining,' she pointed out.

'Is it?' I hadn't noticed.

She shook her head. 'Let's go in the shed.'

I followed and waited for her to get comfortable. Then I started, 'I've just read the news. Over seventy cats have been killed.' Her mouth dropped open in shock. 'We have to do something.'

She still appeared shaken. 'What can we do?' she asked.

'We can find out who it is and we can...' I was hoping she'd fill in the blanks. She remained stubbornly silent, '...scratch them to death!' She raised an eyebrow. Then I had a brilliant idea. 'Ally!'

She shook her head gravely. 'Dogs that attack humans are normally destroyed,' she told me sombrely.

'Are they?'

She nodded. 'Never forget, the humans are in control here. Their behaviour is not always rational.'

'We couldn't do that to Ally,' I agreed. 'We'll have to find another way.'

She stared through the door, watching as the rain intensified. 'First we have to find him,' she mumbled.

We sat in the shed for a long time watching as a storm unfolded. Neither of us wanted to get wet and, although the shed was cold, it was dry and safe. Darkness had overtaken us by the time the storm blew over. We slept through most of it, raising a lazy eyebrow in response to the loudest claps of thunder.

Secret appeared on the patio in front of us, splashing through the puddles. 'Nip!'

I wasted no time on pleasantries. 'We need to speak to Nutter,' I told him.

'She lives up a tree,' he replied.

'I can climb trees.'

'You can't get down again though, can

you?'

There was an element of truth in his assertion. 'Couldn't she come down, just for a few minutes?'

'My kits!' he cried.

'You could stay with them while she talked to us,' Flash suggested.

He squeaked in protest. 'But...!'

'I think you can manage a few minutes,' she told him patiently. 'Come on, let's go. Strike while the iron's hot.'

I didn't know what she meant about hot irons, but followed dutifully. We didn't have far to travel. His tree was at the bottom of my garden, and there were several, convenient overhanging branches. No wonder he was able to appear so silently.

'Go on,' urged Flash, giving his bushy tail a quick bite with her teeth.

'Ow!' He wasn't enthusiastic, but scampered up the trunk anyway.

Some minutes later, a tired looking squirrel with wide hips and a slightly manky tail appeared.

'Nutter!' Flash greeted her. 'How are you?'

'I must be mad,' she replied, nodding at me. 'Leaving him with the children.'

'He'll be fine,' Flash assured her. We all pretended we hadn't heard a short high-pitched squeak.

'What can I do for you?' she asked.

'You saw the cat killer,' Flash reminded her.

'I think so. He was so familiar. Unusually tall.' She bit her lip in concentration. 'He was somebody I'd seen before.'

'Postman?' Flash asked. She shook her head. 'Paperboy?' Same response. 'Delivery man?' No luck. Flash turned to me.

I couldn't think of any more regular callers. 'What about the local paper in the afternoon?'

'He was always carrying something.'

'What?'

'I can't remember. It'll come to me, though.' It was getting more difficult to ignore the shrieking and wailing coming from high above our heads. 'I'd better get back. I'll let you know if I remember anything.'

We thanked her and she dashed away. Seconds later, she was replaced by an untidy Secret. His face was drawn and his fur could have done with a good grooming. There was a patch of hair missing from his tail. 'You didn't have to take so long!' he cried in distress.

'It was two minutes,' I told him.

'Less,' Flash insisted.

'I'll never be the same again! All those little mouths screaming at me, biting me. And the smell!'

'Sounds like you need to instil a bit of discipline,' Flash suggested.

'Discipline,' he muttered, turning away. 'I'm a forager!'

The evening was turning cold. There was no sign of Diamond. Even Ginger had given us a miss. We decided to go home and get warm.

After Lucy had gone to bed, I usually snoozed in the front room while her parents watched TV. On this occasion, I made a point of pushing the local paper off the coffee table and pawing at its front page until I had their attention. Brian, the male human, was the first to pick up on my actions and notice the headline. I looked up at him appealingly. 'I know, Yowl,' he told me. 'It's hard to believe. Better make sure you're tucked up safely in bed every night.'

I yowled in response.

That night I dreamt of Hewt. I'd heard a traffic report on the radio called *Eye in the Sky*. It was exactly what we needed.

I awoke with a beautiful, reddish sky heralding the new day. Of course, most humans missed this glorious display. Cats tended to wake at the first sign of morning light. That way we could get up, go out, do our business, and be back for a snooze before breakfast. I'd heard some humans repeat the phrase *Red sky at night, shepherds' delight. Red sky in the morning, shepherds' warning.* I didn't know any shepherds, so I couldn't warn them.

Lucy showed no sign of the anger she'd displayed the previous evening. Everything was pleasantly harmonious. No-one seemed to be getting ready to go out. It must be the weekend. No school for Lucy. Normally, I would have kept her company, but I felt I had important matters to attend to. I went straight round to see Flash. Diamond was already there, curled up in a ball in the sunshine, snoring lightly. I trod softly. I didn't want to wake him. Flash indicated with her head that we should move away. 'I told him what you discovered yesterday,' she said. 'He's very concerned. He's having a think.'

'Think?' I remarked. 'It looks like he's asl...'

'The lights may be off, but the wheels are turning,' she assured me. When we settled a suitable distance away, she informed me, 'I've been thinking. None of us are normally out at night. We need to enlist the help of the nocturnal creatures. I've left a message for Big Red...'

'Who's he?'

'The leader of the foxes,' she explained.

'Foxes!' I said, alarmed.

'Calm down! He's the boss and he's always been helpful whenever I've asked him anything.'

'Foxes are scary,' I told her.

'No,' she replied calmly. 'They just keep themselves to themselves.'

'Why is that?'

She shook her head. 'I don't know. They're not very sociable.' She took a moment to consider. 'They have big families; they're wonderful parents, too. They just don't choose to mix much.' She saw my apprehensive expression. 'You should come one morning and watch their cubs frolicking on the lawn down the way. They're beautiful.'

'Where do they live?'

'Just past Diamond's house,' she told me. 'There's a bit of scrap land at the end of the houses.'

'And they're up all night?'

'Every night.'

'They must have seen something,' I insisted.

'Yo, Bro! How's it hanging?' Ginger strode purposefully down the lawn. He looked as if he'd spent a lot of time on his coat, which was standing up at a strange angle above his eyes. 'Like the new look?' he asked, evidently proud of himself.

Flash shook her head sadly.

I asked, 'How long did that take you?'

'A few minutes,' he answered dismissively. 'Does it make me look more appealing to the ladies?'

'It makes you look like a porcupine,' she told him.

I thought back to Lucy's *Animals of the World* book. She was right. They had sticky-up spikes. I chuckled involuntarily.

'What's so funny, squirt?' he demanded.

'Porcupines!'

He sat down disgruntled. 'I've never met a porcupine.'

There came what could only be described as a grumbling growl from the bushes at the end of the garden. I was immediately prepared for the worst. All my hair stood on end and my tail flushed up to three times its normal size.

'Ah!' responded Flash calmly. 'Our audience has been granted. Follow me.'

We trailed after her into the rhododendron bushes, which bore pinkish flowers despite the cold weather. Carefully camouflaged amidst a pile of russet leaves, a nose was visible with evil eyes lurking not far behind. I took a step behind Flash's generous bulk. My body reacted to the musky smell of the fox. I couldn't help it. It was a natural cat reaction in the face of a predator. A deep growl was forming in my throat.

Fortunately, Flash was experiencing no such response. 'Red,' she greeted him in an overly friendly manner. 'Thanks for seeing us.'

'It's always a pleasure, for you.' His voice was over-oozing sincerity. He had to be lying.

'How's the family?' she asked.

He raised his eyes. 'A constant trial. The great-great-grandchildren are completely out of control. I told Rusty he was looking for trouble with that girl.'

Flash smiled indulgently. 'She's a good girl. They just do things differently in the country. Life on a farm, you know?'

He nodded in agreement. 'So, who's the new boy? Why's he hiding?'

I peered round Flash's hind quarters. 'I'm Yowl.'

'Pleased to meet you,' he responded politely.

I remained silent. I didn't trust him.

'We wanted to know whether you'd seen the Tall Man on your travels,' Flash explained.

'Who?'

'The cat killer,' I clarified. 'He's killed over

seventy cats already. We have to stop him.'

Red looked straight at me and licked his lips. It felt like he was sizing me up for his breakfast. 'Seventy! I didn't realise it was that bad.'

'Patch saw him once. Bit him! Stopped him killing another one.'

Red smiled and appeared to relax. 'He always was a good boy.' He sat down and asked, 'What do you know about this killer?'

'We call him the Tall Man,' I explained.

'Anything else?'

'He's tall and thin and wears a woolly hat,' Flash informed him.

'And he smells of cat food,' I added.

'Where does he operate?'

'Patch saw him near the school.'

Red grunted. 'I only ever go over that way on a Wednesday. Rubbish bags, you know.'

'Can you spread the word, keep a lookout?' Flash asked. 'We need to know where he lives.'

He nodded gravely. 'I will.'

'But be careful!' she urged. 'He's very dangerous.'

He nodded thoughtfully. 'What will you do

when you find his house?'

I looked at Flash. She looked at me. 'We'll work something out,' I assured him.

He yawned spectacularly. Despite having a couple missing, his teeth looked strong and exceedingly sharp. 'Time for my bed,' he told us. 'I'll make sure everyone's aware. I'll let you know if they see anything.'

Flash thanked him and he strolled leisurely away. 'Told you,' she said. 'He's a fine fellow.'

'He looked like he wanted to eat me.'

She sighed. 'Let's get back to Diamond.'

I agreed enthusiastically. 'Where's Ginger?' I hadn't noticed he'd disappeared.

'I was just...' he blurted, emerging from behind a large tree trunk.

'You were hiding!' I squealed in delight. 'You were scared!'

'Nonsense!' he replied harshly. 'I just needed to lift a leg.'

Flash strolled on ahead in the direction of Diamond's garden. We galloped to catch her. There was no sign of him. Flash walked on and poked her head through the cat flap. 'Hi, Stud,' she remarked. I could hear Diamond groan and Flash disappeared inside. I took a look through and saw Diamond attempting to stretch his front legs. He didn't get very far. 'Are you alright?' Flash asked with evident concern.

'Just...resting my eyes,' came a feeble response.

In contrast to my previous visit, there was no delicious smell permeating the air. He obviously noticed my sniffing and disappointed expression. 'Sorry, kid. I ate it all.' There was obviously nothing wrong with his appetite. 'Didn't know you were coming.'

Flash sat down next to him and told him about the latest developments. 'Hmm...' he responded. 'I need a drink.' He stood with some difficulty and walked on stiff legs to his bowl. He groaned. 'Must have finished it.'

'There's a bowl out here with water,' I told him. I'd investigated it on the way in hoping that it contained salmon.

'Right,' he said and walked slowly outside. He spent some minutes crouched over the bowl drinking.

When he'd finished, a concerned Flash

asked, 'What's the matter, Diamond?'

'Can't seem to... Always thirsty.' So saying, he bent down over the bowl and started to drink again. Eventually, he looked up. His eyes were bloodshot and yellow.

'Can we do anything for you?' Flash asked, her concern evident.

'No, no...' he muttered in response. 'Don't trouble...'

'It's no trouble,' she insisted. 'I want you to be comfortable.'

'Well, maybe you could stay with me for a while.'

'Of course! I'd be happy to.' She gestured with her head towards Ginger and me, suggesting we leave.

'See you later, Diamond,' I called as we left. When we were at a safe distance, I remarked. 'Didn't look good, did he?'

'He has a kidney problem,' he explained. 'It flares up every now and then. He'll be alright in a day or two.'

'Getting old really sucks, huh?'

He nodded thoughtfully.

We returned home, promising to meet up

again later. In the event, I got caught up reading with Lucy and forgot all about it.

5

Scene of a Crime

The following morning, when I ventured outside, everything was quiet. I chased a few sparrows, who chirped at me in indignation. Of course, I never caught one. Ginger appeared and we attempted an ambitious pincer movement that almost resulted in success. But not quite. We both sat back panting.

A great fluttering announced the arrival of Digger. He landed heavily on the lawn. I wondered what it was like to be able to fly. 'You'll never guess what I just heard,' he told us breathlessly.

'What?' Ginger prompted, not displaying any great interest.

'I'm not sure I should tell you,' he went on.

'OK!' Ginger remarked and walked away.

Everything I'd previously heard about pigeons suggested he wouldn't be able to keep it to himself. 'Just tell us.'

He came closer and leaned his head towards us. 'You know Snort?' he whispered conspiratorially.

I looked at Ginger. He shook his head. 'No,' I told him.

He tutted impatiently. 'One of the young foxes.'

'One of Red's great-great-grandchildren?'

He took a moment to work it through his pigeon brain. 'No!' he exclaimed with a measure of certainty. 'A great-grandchild, I think.' He looked pleased with himself. 'A different generation entirely.'

'Right!' I responded. 'His partner is a girl from the country?'

He looked dumbfounded. 'Really?'

I shook my head impatiently. 'What about him?'

'He's hurt. He came home with an injury to his flank and bruises to his head.' He shook his head sadly. 'They're not sure he'll survive.'

'How did it happen?' I asked in shock.

'They don't know. He collapsed as soon as he arrived. He hasn't been able to say anything.'

'Red must be very angry,' I suggested.

'You can say that again. He's seething!'

'How...?' I attempted to ask, but his giant wings were already beating.

'Got to go!' he squawked back at us. 'More people to tell...'

I looked at Ginger. 'I wonder...'

He nodded. 'Sounds familiar.'

'We should pay them a visit,' I suggested.

His mouth dropped open. 'Are you insane?'

'They won't hurt us,' I assured him.

'You remember it was only yesterday that Flash asked them to look out for the Tall Man. What if Snort found him?'

'Then... We'd be a step closer to identifying him.'

'But what if Snort tried to follow him home and was attacked on the way?'

'Then we could narrow down where he lives,' I suggested.

'You're missing the point!' he hissed. 'He wouldn't have followed him if Flash hadn't asked.'

It began to dawn on me. 'If Flash hadn't asked, he wouldn't have been hurt.'

'Yes!'

I shook my head. 'It doesn't matter,' I insisted with more certainty than I felt. 'Red agreed to help. He could have said no. I'm going to see him. Coming?'

'We should wait for Flash,' he suggested.

'You know Diamond's sick. She won't leave him.'

He obviously didn't want to, but tagged along a few steps behind. I wasn't sure where they lived, but it wasn't difficult to follow my nose. The musky smell intensified and I had difficulty stopping my body adopting a natural defensive bearing. As we approached a mass of what looked like garden refuse, two sentry foxes stood to attention on either side, growling menacingly. A pale fox with a twitching nose approached us between the sentries. 'State your business,' he growled. He licked his lips as he looked at me from top to bottom.

I took a deep breath and tried to sound assertive. 'I'd like to speak to Mr Red, please.'

'Concerning what?'

'I spoke with him yesterday,' I told him. 'I heard about Snort. I'm worried.'

He gave me a contemptuous look. He apparently didn't consider me much of a threat. 'Wait.' He marched off under the seat of what looked like an old garden chair.

Some minutes later, Red strolled out. He came towards me and stopped inches away, nose to nose. 'Yowl, isn't it?'

'That's right, sir. And this is Ging...' I looked around. He'd disappeared again.

'Looks like you're all alone,' he remarked with a wicked grin, revealing his sharp teeth.

I gulped, but carried on regardless. 'I heard about Snort. I thought it might be the Tall Man. Will he be alright?'

'He died a few minutes ago,' he informed me.

I gasped. 'I'm so sorry,' I blustered. 'I had no idea.'

He sighed. 'He was too weak.'

'Did he say anything?'

He shook his head. 'He didn't have the strength.' He thought for a moment before continuing, 'His injury was very clean. No animal made that wound. I don't know how he managed to get back home. He didn't want to die alone, I think.'

I lowered my head as was customary on these occasions. 'Are you angry with us?' I asked with some trepidation.

'With you, no!' he replied emphatically. 'With the person who did it, yes! Very!'

'But...'

'Listen kid,' he told me, settling down. 'You're young. You have a lot to learn,' he explained me more patiently than I would have expected under the circumstances. I nodded in agreement. 'When Flash told me someone's killing cats, as far as I'm concerned, someone's killing foxes too. Understand?'

I shook my head. I was confused. 'No.'

'We animals stick together. If we're in some sort of danger, everyone helps out. It doesn't matter whether it's a dog with rabies, a cat with cat flu, or a madman with a knife, it affects us all. We foxes aren't your enemy. You can rely on us to help whenever you need us.' He licked his lips again in the manner that made me nervous. 'It wasn't so long ago that one of our youngsters went missing. You know who?' he asked. I shook my head. 'It was

Snort. A few years ago now, when he was a cub. We searched all night. Couldn't find him anywhere. We put the word out and you know who found him? Diamond! He'd got himself trapped in a shed, crying his heart out, he was. Couldn't get out! Diamond got in somehow and brought him home. He carried him all the way back here by the scruff of his neck.'

'Really?'

'I'll never forget that.'

'Wow!'

'We might not be too sociable, but we stick together, kid,' he muttered. 'We're finding out where Snort was attacked. Two of my sons are following the trail. It might help. This human's a danger to all of us.'

I nodded. 'He certainly is.'

'Thanks for coming,' he told me. 'I'll let you know what we find.'

'Thank you.'

He turned away and addressed his sentries. 'This is Yowl,' he explained. 'If he wants to see me, it's fine. Let him in.'

They nodded in response. All that was missing was a salute. I wandered away, expecting Ginger to jump out from behind a nearby tree, but he was nowhere to be seen. I didn't want to disturb Diamond. He needed his rest. I trudged miserably back home.

Lucy was upstairs doing her homework. I jumped on her desk and checked the subject: geography. I wasn't sure that would be helpful to me, but I snuggled down anyway. *What is the capital of Spain?* was the first question. That was easy enough: Madrid. I licked an irritating itch on my foreleg, wondering where I'd acquired that information. Someone must have told me. Then I remembered. The adults had been watching a quiz show on television. Geography was one of the subjects. It seemed like once I'd heard something, it stuck in my brain. I didn't even remember the question, but I knew the answer. Instant recall. I was proud of myself.

I snoozed through the evening, waking just long enough to eat my dinner. Then I curled up on the windowsill and listened as the house fell silent. I'd had a good day. I'd had an introduction to the foxes and ended up on good terms with their leader. Not only that, I'd learned a lot. I'd learned not to prejudge other animals. When all was said and done, the animals stood united, against anyone or any animal that threatened our safety.

I fell asleep with a smile on my face.

*

The next morning, the first thought on my mind was Diamond. I was worried. I'd hardly recognised the broken figure we'd encountered the previous day, unable to quench his thirst no matter how much he drank. I ate a few fish biscuits and then strolled down the garden, encountering Secret sniffing around the base of our apple tree.

'Morning!' I called.

'Morning, Yowl,' he returned.

'What are you doing?' I asked.

'I'm sure I buried some nuts around here,' he answered, frantically sniffing. 'The youngsters are hungry.'

I cast my mind back to the kitchen fruit bowl: I thought I could remember some overripe grapes and an apple that was definitely past its sell-by date. The apple I'd struggle to carry, but I could manage some more grapes. I brought him a branch looking significantly less green than previously. He gave them a wary sniff when he saw them. 'Are they alright?' he asked.

'I don't know. I don't eat grapes. Ask Nutter,' I suggested.

He took the stem in his teeth and departed. I walked across to Flash's garden. I nosed around but there was no sign of her, so I headed for Diamond's house. I squeezed under the fence at the end of the garden and immediately saw Flash and Diamond together on the patio. I galloped the short distance and greeted them warmly. 'Good to see you up and about,' I told Diamond.

'Yes,' he replied. 'I'm feeling a little better today. Comes and goes, you know.'

'Your eyes don't look so yellow,' I told him.

He nodded. 'I'll be right as rain in a couple of days.' He took a deep breath. 'So, what did you get up to yesterday?'

'I went to see Red.'

'On your own?' Flash asked in shock.

'Well, I went with Ginger but he...disappeared.'

They shared a glance. I got the impression neither were very surprised. 'That was brave of you,' Diamond told me.

'I wanted to see how Snort was.'

'And how is he?'

'He died.'

'Oh,' he groaned in distress.

'Red told me about you finding him when he was a kid.'

He nodded wearily. 'Little terror, was Snort. Always poking his nose in where it wasn't wanted.'

'Red said the wound was very clean. Not something any animal could inflict.'

'So it *was* the Tall Man,' Flash confirmed.

I nodded. 'Red sent two of his sons to follow the trail, find out where it happened.'

'Good!' Diamond nodded in approval. 'Let's go and see what they found.'

'Not you, Stud!' Flash told him. 'You're staying right here, back in your bed. I'll go with Yowl and we'll talk to you later.'

Diamond struggled to control his disappointment, but he accepted that Flash was right. He snuggled down in his basket and closed his eyes.

'Coming?' she asked over her shoulder as she strolled up the garden.

I chased after her and soon we were approaching the sentry foxes. They stood on guard as usual, but as I approached, they lowered their heads and allowed us to pass. Flash showed her approval with a quiet purr. We stood in front of the dilapidated garden chair and waited. Within seconds, Red's nose appeared. He recognised us and stepped out. 'Hiya, kid! Thought I might see you again.' He nodded a greeting towards Flash.

'I was sorry to hear about Snort,' she responded.

Red lowered his head in the appropriate fashion. 'It's not like him to get caught. He was quick, crafty.' He met her eyes. 'I intend to find out what happened.'

'Good! We'll help in any way we can.'

He nodded slowly. 'I know.'

'What did your sons find?' I asked.

'It happened just the other side of the

school,' he told us. I exchanged a glance with Flash.

'That's where Patch bit him when he was attacking a cat.' He raised his eyebrows. 'It seems to be where he operates,' I finished with.

'I'll post some sentries. They can keep watch at night.' He thought for a few moments. 'It would be good for you to visit the scene,' he told us. 'There were two buttons by a fence. We didn't touch them, disturb the scent. You might get something.'

Flash nodded slowly. 'We could take Ally. He never forgets a scent.'

'Good idea,' he agreed. 'Now?'

Flash looked around. 'Why not?'

We set off with two of his sons flanking him, Dash and Creeper. We picked up Ally on the way. Technically, he was supposed to stay in his garden. They had strong fences to ensure that he did. However, Alsatians are very good at jumping and the fence provided no real barrier. He simply jumped over the top.

We travelled further than I'd ever been before. I tried to keep track of the streets, but they all looked the same after a while. Red and

Flash seemed to know where they were going, but everything merged into a single, vast panorama for me. Streets of red brick houses with no pavements were quickly followed by roads crammed with blocks of concrete flats. Each had its own distinctive scent. Even the streetlights changed as we progressed. The older streets had yellow lights, while the newer ones were white. On the streets with pavements, small trees were planted at regular intervals. I couldn't begin to explain the foul smell from the soil at their base. I think there were a lot of pet dogs in the area.

Eventually, we stopped at a safe distance from a patch of pavement discoloured with rusty patches. The area was saturated with a distinctive scent, even though it wasn't recent. 'The buttons are over here,' Red told us, leading us closer to the fence, where two identical buttons lay. They were small and black with four holes through the centre in a square formation. We all stood back as Ally approached. An Alsatian's nose is exquisitely sensitive, even by animal standards. He took in three deep breaths through his big nostrils, then stood back and nodded. Once a scent was registered in his brain, he'd never forget it. Flash and I followed his lead. We knelt and sniffed, clearly discerning human, alongside that of fox.

'There's something else,' Ally informed us. We all looked up eagerly. 'Cat!' he whispered.

'Go on,' urged Red.

'A *scared* cat,' he explained. 'Young, like you,' he said, pointing his nose at me. 'A female.'

Something fleeting caught my eye and I instinctively turned my head. Halfway down a footpath, from amidst towering foliage, we were being watched. 'We've got company,' I whispered to Red.

Without moving his head, his eyes moved in the direction I indicated. 'Hmm,' he muttered, before dispatching his sons in the opposite direction. As soon as they were out of sight, they broke into a sprint and disappeared into different front gardens. We continued to chat as though nothing had happened. The nose remained partially concealed in the bushes. Within a minute, the imposing figure of Dash appeared at the other end of the pathway, blocking the exit. Between the twitching nose and us, another path branched off. Almost instantaneously, Creeper stationed himself at the junction, just out of sight. It was a classic manoeuvre. Our observer would see the encroaching Dash and look to flee up the path. Then Creeper would take a single step forward and leave them with nowhere to go.

Red gave the slightest nod and Dash began taking steady steps down the alley towards us, making no attempt to keep quiet. After about four steps, I saw the nervous nose switch direction. It saw the oncoming fox and desperately swung its head from side to side seeking an escape route. It didn't wait until Dash was too close before breaking cover and heading for the side path. What emerged was a small dappled cat, a mix of every cat colour, apparently painted at random. I say small, but she was probably about the same size as me. One thing was certain: she was terrified. She got within a few paces of the perpendicular pathway. Then Creeper stepped forward. He made no move towards her. He just sat, blocking the path. Frantic, she looked one way then the other.

She saw there was no escape and sank down in defeat, trying to make herself look as small as possible.

Red nodded at me. 'I think you'd better handle this. She's scared enough already.'

I took a deep breath and stepped forward. She was a pathetic sight and my heart went out to her. No creature should have cause to be that terrified. I approached her in an unthreatening way and stopped a couple of paces away. In her current state, she might lash out at anything or anyone. 'There's no need to be scared. We mean you no harm,' I started gently. 'My name's Yowl, what's yours?'

She looked at me with terror in her eyes. She was scared and didn't trust anyone. I could hear a growl rumbling in her throat.

'We're trying to find out what happened here yesterday,' I told her. 'You were here, weren't you?' I asked hopefully. Out of the corner of my eye, I saw Ally nodding in confirmation. She was indeed our eye witness.

'F-f-f-foxes!' she exclaimed in obvious horror.

'They're my friends,' I told her calmly.

'They won't hurt you.'

'Y-y-yesterday, one tried to eat me,' she told me.

'Why don't you tell me what happened?'

'I was hungry.'

I nodded. 'And a man gave you food.'

'Yes. Then he picked me up.'

'You let him?'

'No!' she shrieked. 'He took me by surprise. I was eating and he grabbed me by the scruff of my neck. I couldn't move.'

'Then what happened?'

'It was all so quick! I think he wanted to stroke me. His hand came round and then this fox was leaping up, straight for me, with his mouth wide open.' She had a quick think to refresh her mind. 'I could see his teeth. They were huge!'

'But he didn't bite you?'

'No. The man's hand got in the way and he bit his wrist instead. He cried out and dropped me. I ran away and when I turned back, the fox still had his arm in his mouth. Then the man did something. I thought he hit him. The fox shrieked and let go of his arm. Then he limped away.'

'What happened to the man?'

'He walked away. He was holding his arm. I think it was really hurting.'

'Which way did he walk?'

She indicated with her nose. 'Up there.'

I sat down in front of her, keeping very calm. I didn't want to unnerve her now. 'That man who picked you up. We call him the Tall Man. He kills cats,' I explained. 'He attracts them with food. Then he kills them.'

She took in a sharp breath.

'You were going to be next. The fox stopped him. He saved your life.'

Her mouth opened wide in surprise as she ran through the events in her mind again. 'But...' she started.

Flash crept over very slowly and took her place beside me. 'He's right. This man is very dangerous. You had a lucky escape.'

'But...'

'We have to stop him.'

She looked across at Red, who'd also crept a few paces closer in order to hear clearer. 'That fox yesterday, is he...?'

Red nodded slowly. 'He was my great-grandson. He died of his injuries.'

She looked at me. I nodded to confirm Red's story. 'He saved me?' she asked him.

'That's right. We stand together: foxes and cats...and dogs,' Red added, remembering Ally was present. 'We're not your enemy. You need something, all you have to do is ask.'

'I always thought...'

He shook his head. 'I'm afraid we're not very sociable. We like to stay with our families. We don't mix much, but you'll never be in any danger from us.'

She was silent.

'Feel like telling us your name yet?' I asked.

She almost broke into a smile. I think it was mostly from relief. 'I'm called Shadow,' she told us.

'Nice name,' I replied.

'They said it was because I was afraid of my own. Shadow, I mean.'

'But not anymore?'

'No!' She rose to her full height. She wasn't tall, but she had a lovely face and a lithe body. It looked like she could do with a good meal.

'You have a home?' Flash asked.

'Not really. I sleep in one of the sheds down the way.'

'Why don't you come back with us,' Flash suggested. 'I'm sure we can find you some food.'

'Really? I'm starving.'

Flash nodded. 'This man,' she went on. 'What did he look like?'

She thought back. 'He was tall and thin. He had a black hat on. Long, straight nose. I couldn't see his hair.' It was better than nothing, but would hardly distinguish him from thousands of others. 'I could smell food.'

We began the long journey home. I made it my business to stay very close to Shadow. She didn't need any more surprises. Diamond had a shed she could use for as long as she needed. I whispered that he usually had more food than he could eat, so she wouldn't go hungry. I liked her. Despite her naturally timid nature, she had guts. I remembered the way she'd growled and spat at us when we'd approached to speak. Yet she had the intelligence to understand the truth of what we were explaining to her.

We dropped off Ally, thanking him for his help. He assured us that if we needed anything else, he'd be ready and willing. Then we reached the home of the foxes. As the three of them stepped away from us, Shadow piped up in a weak voice, 'I'm sorry about your great-grandson.'

Red turned back with a very calm expression. He nodded twice then disappeared under the chair.

We followed on to bring Diamond up to date with the day's developments. He grunted his approval. We all knew that the next time the foxes spotted the Tall Man they'd lay low and follow him home. Maybe we wouldn't need Hewt's help after all.

'Yo! Shadow!' came a cry from a distance. Apparently, Ginger was already familiar with our new acquaintance.

She turned away from him and pulled a face. She evidently wasn't impressed. 'Ginger,' she greeted him as he approached.

'What you doin' here, girl?'

'We were meeting the foxes,' she told him.

'Foxes!' he squawked.

'They're our friends,' she told him patiently.

'Yeah, yeah, I know,' he mumbled, trying to cover his shock. 'Me and Yowl paid them a visit yesterday,' he said without any hint of embarrassment.

'About that...' I started.

'Yeah, I know,' he interrupted. 'Had to run an errand. Very urgent. Sorry!'

'You left Yowl to face them alone,' Diamond pointed out in his gruff voice.

'It's cool,' he assured him. 'The foxes are our friends,' he repeated, like a mantra

Diamond grunted. He knew exactly what had happened and was clearly unimpressed.

'I'm a player!' Ginger insisted. 'I had things to do!'

'Like trying to find the Tall Man?' Flash suggested.

'Yeah, exactly like that. I was trying to get a message to Hewt.'

'And how did you propose to do that?' Flash enquired.

'I was talking to Digger.'

'Digger!' we all exclaimed.

'That's right. He said he'd fly up and have a word with him.'

'Digger?' Flash asked. 'The same Digger who's so fat he can hardly get off the ground?'

'I've seen him above the treetops,' Ginger insisted defensively.

'He's probably already forgotten,' Diamond added.

'Digger flew south today,' a voice announced at breakneck speed. 'He's visiting relatives... If he can remember where they live.'

We all looked up and saw Secret hanging upside down from a branch. 'Squirrels can climb trees,' I pointed out.

He took a visible gulp. 'Small trees!'

'Tall trees are just small trees that have grown a bit,' Diamond proposed philosophically.

'I can't...!' He stuttered. 'I get a nose bleed when I get near the top of our tree.'

We all looked at his middle-aged apple tree. It wasn't very high. Every apple could be harvested with a modest ladder. 'A squirrel that's afraid of heights?' I pondered.

'Well...' he started, giving himself time to

formulate a coherent response. 'I'm hanging upside down from a branch, right?' We all nodded. 'What would happen if I fell down?'

'You'd hurt yourself.'

'Exactly!' he cried. 'But not seriously. The grass is nice and soft. Maybe a twisted ankle or a bruised thigh, but I'd be fine in a few days.' He took an exaggerated look up the full height of the magnificent pine tree. 'Don't forget, Hewt isn't exactly welcoming visitors recently. What if I said "Hello" and he flies out at me clawing my eyeballs?'

'You'd fall down?'

'Yes, I'd fall down. And what would happen if I fell down from up there?'

'You'd die,' I suggested.

'Yes! Then who'd forage for food for my babies?'

'I would,' responded Flash immediately.

'You would?'

'Of course. You really think we'd let your kits starve after you'd made the ultimate sacrifice?'

'Besides, Nutter's very resourceful,' Diamond added. 'She'd probably forget all about you in a couple of days.'

'That's very comforting!' he replied sarcastically. 'I think you're missing the point: I'd be dead!'

'It's for the greater good,' Diamond told him.

'All we want to do is contact Hewt,' I assured him.

'Cats can climb trees,' he told me defensively.

I took another look at that tall, slender trunk. 'We can't get down again, though,' I reminded him.

'Well, you seem to think it's appropriate for me to sacrifice myself, why doesn't one of you?'

We all looked at each other. Diamond and Flash were obviously too old, Ginger... Ginger would probably agree to do it and then remember something more important, and Shadow simply wasn't strong enough. That left me... I swallowed loudly.

'We'll have to wait and see whether Red's troops come up with anything,' Diamond stated just as I was getting seriously worried. 'With luck, they'll find him in a day or two.'

But they didn't.

Not only that, more *Missing* posters appeared on nearby lampposts and fences.

The local paper featured more articles and interviewed several heartbroken owners.

Digger returned from his travels and brought news of more victims being discovered in distant locations. The Tall Man's patch was growing wider. Despite everything, homeless cats were still being enticed into his clutches by the simple promise of food. The foxes helped to institute a primitive food bank for hungry cats at night. We all gave up part of our food, which they distributed during their nocturnal travels. We were doing all we could, but until someone, or something, was able to identify the culprit, all we could do was fight fires. We needed to stop the man responsible for providing the initial spark. The foxes were out every night, but so far hadn't encountered him.

We were all agreed.

We needed Hewt.

6

A Narrow Escape

That night I didn't sleep.

I came to the conclusion that all our hopes rested on me.

I didn't even know whether I could make it to the top of such a tall tree.

If I got to the top and found Hewt's nest, what would I do then? Even if I could convince him to help us, how could I possibly get back down the tree? *Just lead down with your front paws as far as you can go, then jump and land on your feet,* Ginger had told me. I hadn't even mastered that. The chances were that if I *could* get to speak to Hewt, I wouldn't be alive to discover whether or not it had helped. I spent a long time thinking through my options. As I watched the dawn breaking, I realised I didn't have any.

As soon as the birds started chattering, I set out, long before Flash and Diamond would wake up. I took a lingering look around the garden. I might never see it again. It hadn't been my home for long, but I liked it. Everything was made comfortable for me: my humans were kind and affectionate and most importantly, they fed me regularly. My neighbours were great role models for me and I enjoyed spending time with them. Every way I'd turned, I'd found friends. Nothing I'd found in my world was hostile. The Tall Man inhabited the same landscape, but I'd been lucky enough not to encounter him. And there, in a nutshell, was why I was standing at the base of the highest pine tree in the area: to preserve our comfortable animal way of life.

I took a look overhead. High up where the branches began to get thinner, there was a solid mass of sticks and leaves and everything else Hewt had needed to build a nest. A nest for his family. A nest that he now inhabited alone. The first branch looked almost as high as our two-storey house. I'd have to reach that level before I'd be able to take a rest. I wished I'd had more practice climbing trees, but if I had, I might not have had the courage.

I took a few steps back. If I was going to do this, I might as well do it properly. I launched myself at the trunk and when I was a good stride away, I leapt as high as I could, impaling the bark with my claws and pulling myself up with my front legs, pushing off with my hind legs. I made impressive progress. I raced upwards and I could see the distance to the branch rapidly diminishing. Unfortunately, as I approached it, I felt a searing pain in my right shoulder that brought me to an immediate stop. I gripped the trunk with my three functioning paws and desperately flexed my right foreleg. It slowly began to respond. It must have been a touch of cramp. I couldn't stay where I was without falling. Using my hind legs to push me a stride at a time, I hauled myself onto the branch. It was wide enough for me to sit and rest my limbs.

I was already panting.

I could feel my heart beating more rapidly that I could ever recall. I tried to control my breathing. I made the mistake of taking another look up. There was so far to go, but the branches swiftly became more regular, which meant more chances to rest. Then I made a bigger mistake and looked down. I felt nauseous. I noticed something moving but didn't wait to identify it. I had no intention of looking down again.

'Yowl!' came a faint cry from below.

I yowled in response.

'Don't do it! Stay where you are.' It was a deep voice, clearly Diamond's. 'My humans have a ladder. They can help you down. If you go any higher, they won't be able to reach you.'

Making sure I was well-balanced close to the trunk, I glanced down. He and Flash were sitting at the base of the tree, staring up. 'Come back, Yowl!' cried Flash. She sounded desperate.

'I have to do this,' I shouted down at them. 'There's no other way!'

There was a resounding silence. I think they both realised I was right. The good news was that I was slowly regaining the feeling in my right foreleg. I flexed it and rotated it. I was confident that after a short rest, I'd be able to continue. I gazed up again. At a conservative estimate, I was a quarter of the way up and I was already struggling, but I was young and fit. I'd find hidden reserves of energy when the time came, or so I hoped.

After a few minutes, I tried my front leg. Everything had returned to near-normal. There was still a hint of a dull ache, but nothing to restrict its function. I took a few paces backwards, careful not to lose my balance. Then, once again, I raced towards the trunk and leapt as high as I could, using my claws to propel me upwards. Front and rear legs were perfectly synchronised and I made rapid progress. Then I began to flag. I took a couple of final strides and hauled myself onto the next convenient branch. It was noticeably narrower than the previous one. I didn't venture far from the trunk. The branch was too narrow. I tried to sit to gather my strength but soon found that the only way I could do that was with my back against the trunk. I was careful not to look down. I could no longer hear Diamond and Flash. I glanced upwards. The nest still appeared a long way away.

This time, my body felt different. When I'd stopped on the lower branch, I felt fine, just out of breath. This time, the effort had resulted in a genuine feeling of fatigue, mental as well as physical. I was struggling to assess the distance I'd covered. I didn't feel inclined to look down. I knew I still had a long way to go and I didn't rush myself. Already, I was beyond the point of no return. I couldn't climb down and no ladder would be able to reach me. I only had one chance and I intended to get it right. I wished there was a handy puddle. I was thirsty.

When I felt as good as I was going to get, I set off again. I took a couple of careful steps backwards and launched myself at the trunk. My flying leaps were getting shorter, but I dug in and propelled myself upwards. When I began to feel tired, I went again, using my hind legs more than my front. I no longer had the energy to pull myself up. My shoulders ached. I had to push with my rear legs. Progress was noticeably slower, but I kept my pushes regular and travelled what I thought was a good distance. Then I found a branch and rested uneasily, my back against the trunk once more, my claws embedded in the bark.

This time, I wasn't panting, I was taking painfully long, deep breaths. It seemed that no amount of inhaling could provide enough oxygen to my hungry lungs. My muscles were trembling and I felt weak as a small kitten. I'd need more than a couple of minutes to recover this time. I rested my head against the tree trunk and tried to regulate my breathing. By leaning back against the tree, I was positioned facing upwards. There it was! Hewt's nest was just a couple of branches away. When I'd started my ascent, I'd have thought nothing of the short distance remaining. Now, in my present state, it would take everything I had left.

I don't know how long I stayed on that meagre branch, clinging on for dear life. Long enough to almost fall asleep a couple of times. Each time my head dropped involuntarily, I shook myself back to my senses before I lost my footing. Eventually, I recovered as much strength as I was going to get. I was fortified by having seen that I was closing in on my target. One more effort and I'd be there.

I stepped back with exaggerated care. The branch bent! I nearly lost my balance. Branches at this height were far narrower than lower down. I dug my claws in and clung on tight, lowering my body closer to the branch. I didn't want to look down. If I fell from this height, it would be a disaster. I summoned up all my remaining strength for one final push.

Previously, I'd raced at the tree trunk. This time it was more of a tired lope that didn't gain much in the way of height. The branch wouldn't support a full leap. I soon discovered that my front legs simply couldn't carry my weight anymore. I took long hesitant strides upwards, propelled by my hind legs alone. My front paws were only good for providing stability. My hind legs were beginning to shake, reluctant to obey my commands, when my head came into contact with a solid mass. It wasn't a branch. It was Hewt's nest and there was a branch perpendicular to that on which it was perched. I hauled myself onto it with the very last of my strength. I held on as it sagged beneath my weight.

I stayed still, unwilling to risk moving, while keeping a wary eye on the nest. I wasn't sure what to expect. I'd never seen a live owl before. I couldn't see Hewt or any activity, but I was prepared for the worst. I knew he wasn't inviting visitors and I had no idea how he'd respond. I spent some time resting. My limbs really did feel dead. I wasn't sure I could take another step.

Fortunately, I didn't have to.

I cleared my throat noisily and waited for a response. Nothing stirred. I hoped I hadn't managed to climb all the way up only to find that he'd moved home. I cleared my throat again, louder this time, and was rewarded by two ears popping up over the nest's wall.

'Wha...?' came a muffled scream, followed by a large owl appearing and shrieking, 'Aaah!' and flapping his wings threateningly.

Involuntarily, I jumped backwards. I couldn't help myself. The branch dipped alarmingly. I lost my balance and only just managed to jab in my front claws before I fell. There I was, hanging by my front claws from a thin branch hundreds of feet above the ground. I heard a scary sound: wood creaking. The branch wasn't strong enough. It was going to give way. I felt defeated. I tried vainly to hook my rear legs over the branch, something simple for a cat in normal life. I couldn't do it. One of my claws flicked out of the bark. It wasn't as strong as below. Then another worked loose. There was nothing I could do. I was falling. I took a last look up at Hewt. He appeared concerned but completely immobile. He was just standing there watching my final desperate attempts to keep hold of a breaking branch.

'Help!' I appealed.

He waddled to the edge of his nest, put his head to one side and said simply, 'Fall!'

It appeared that he still wasn't ready to welcome visitors. I'd come all this way for nothing. Flash and Diamond had been right. I should have stayed on the ground. It's where cats belong. My remaining claws began subtly shifting, scratching the bark as my hanging weight pulled them free. One by one, they disengaged. I tried scratching frantically, but suddenly, there was no branch. I was in free fall, gaining speed as I fell. I watched as the branch above me became smaller and smaller. Then I realigned my body as cats do, feet downwards, ready for a very rough landing. I wondered how long I'd fall. I'd climbed higher than I'd ever been before, but coming down was a whole lot quicker than going up. I watched as branches flew past. Fortunately, I avoided them, although some were very close.

Then something thudded into my back with a loud smack. Immediately, I felt pain along my flanks: intense pain, like being stabbed. Then I was slowing down. I watched as the tree disappeared behind me, travelling at breakneck speed away from the trunk and the obstacles. I was flying! I was hovering above the ground, describing wide arcs over rooftops and gardens. 'Wow!' I cried. I saw my garden passing beneath me as I completed another circle, slowly getting closer to the ground. I couldn't help but let out a loud yowl as I passed over the heads of Diamond and Flash. They stared up at me, transfixed.

All too soon, I was brushing the tops of the fruit trees in neighbouring gardens. I skimmed over the fence and landed gracefully no more than a yard from Diamond and Flash. Shadow rushed out of the shed and brushed forcefully against me. They all broke into huge smiles of relief at my safe return. 'That was very brave, kid,' Diamond told me with admiration in his voice.

'Or very stupid,' Flash added. A predictable response from a mother. She strode towards me purposefully. I thought I was in for a scolding. I'd risked my life climbing the tallest tree in the neighbourhood. Alright, I hadn't managed to have a conversation with Hewt, but she had to be impressed with the way I'd flown down from the treetops and landed a mere hop away from her. I wondered how I'd managed to glide down so smoothly, avoiding all the obstacles in my way. I thought she should have been less angry and more impressed.

I was girding my loins for the full force of her onslaught when she walked straight past me. 'Hewt!' she cried, bumping noses with enough force to knock him backwards. 'We've missed you!'

He chuckled. 'I've had a tough time,' he explained. 'Diamond! How are you doing?'

Diamond approached Hewt with great

enthusiasm. 'Oh, not so bad. I have the odd tough day, you know?'

'Don't we all?' Hewt responded with another grin. 'So, who's the crazy kid?'

I turned and everything became clear. When Hewt had told me to fall, he had every intention of catching me. He could see that I couldn't hang on. It was the only option. And caught me he had, quite painfully actually. 'My name's Yowl, sir,' I started. 'And we need to talk to you.'

'How did you know I was going to bring you back?' he asked.

'I didn't,' I replied. 'I didn't know what to expect.'

He thought for several moments. 'Sorry I scared you,' he told me. 'My wings get terrible cramp squashed in the nest. I had to stretch them.'

I nodded. 'I thought you were going to attack me!'

'Why would I do that?'

'Well,' I started diplomatically. 'People said you weren't too friendly anymore.'

He lowered his head marginally. 'I guess

that's true enough,' he admitted. 'You have no idea how many times I've wished things could have been different.'

'You coped the best way you could,' Diamond told him. 'We understood.'

Hewt nodded. 'And now we have a new generation,' he went on, looking in my direction. 'One of yours?' he asked Flash.

'He is now,' she replied, her voice filled with pride.

Hewt nodded in thought. 'My niece paid me a visit last week. Amazing how she's grown... Soon to be a mother herself. She told me it was time...'

'Time for what?' asked Flash.

'Time to start living again.' He looked up at the sky. 'It's been too long.'

'What happened?' asked Shadow, who evidently hadn't heard the story.

We all went very quiet. Hewt fastened his gaze on Shadow. 'Who are you, little one?' he asked with a smile.

'They call me Shadow,' she told him.

He nodded sagely before retelling his story. 'My partner... My love... My life, was destroyed by some deranged animal, for no reason at all.'

'Oh!' she breathed quietly. 'I'm so sorry!'

He took a deep breath.

I wanted to make sure he didn't still hold the cats responsible. 'Diamond and Flash told me about it,' I explained. 'It didn't sound like the work of a cat to me,' I suggested hesitantly.

'No!' he replied emphatically. 'It was no cat. I tracked down the animal responsible and made sure he'd never hurt another beautiful creature.'

We all went very quiet again. I think we all wanted to know who had done this terrible thing but were too shy to ask. Shadow had no such reticence. 'Who was it?' she asked.

'A wolf!' he informed her.

'Wolf! There are no wolves here... are there?' she gasped.

'There was one,' he went on. 'Some misguided human attempted to keep it as a pet.' He shook his head. 'It could never end well. The wolf escaped and... Princess was not the only casualty.'

'What happened to it?' I asked.

He hesitated before answering, 'I made

sure it would never *see* any more creatures to harm.' We all looked at each other again. His answer was oblique but left me in little doubt what had become of the wolf. 'So, what's so important that this young cat would risk his life for it?'

He listened intently for the next ten minutes while Diamond and Flash brought him up to date with recent events. He asked pertinent questions and prompted when he wanted to hear more. He gave the impression that he possessed immense wisdom and was calculating all the possibilities. When he had no more questions, Flash asked, 'Have you seen him?'

'Probably,' he replied. 'I've seen a man who fits the description giving food to cats. I haven't hung around long enough to see what happened after.'

'You have good eyesight, right?' I asked.

'The best,' he replied modestly.

'Hewt can see a baby dormouse in a field when he's flying above all the trees,' Diamond informed me.

'Wow!' My sides were beginning to throb. I winced as the pain intensified.

Hewt regarded me with a smile. 'Adrenaline beginning to wear off, huh?'

I didn't understand the question. 'What?'

'Adrenaline hides the pain when you're excited. I had to hold you pretty tight and my talons are like razors.'

'It hurts!' I told him.

He shrugged. 'Better to take the pain than the alternative.'

I groaned. I knew he was right but it didn't help mask the pain. Shadow began sniffing at my wounds. I could see blood on my coat. Softly, she began to lick the pain away. She started on one side then I changed my position and she did the same on the other side. When she'd finished, I was almost asleep.

'It's what you need, youngster, after that climb,' Hewt told me. 'That was epic!' he tried to stifle a yawn. 'It's long past my bed time,' he announced. 'I have to get my head down if I'm going to be on the hunt tonight!' He flexed his majestic wings.

'Good to see you again, Hewt,' Diamond told him as he lifted off.

'We missed you!' shouted Flash to his departing back.

'Hey!' came the familiar voice of Ginger, rushing down the garden. 'Was that Hewt?'

'It was,' Diamond told him.

'Aw! I miss all the fun!' he grumbled.

'Maybe if you'd climbed his tree and met with him, you wouldn't have missed it,' Diamond suggested.

'Climb his...!' he scoffed. He noticed a number of sombre faces. 'You don't mean...?'

'Yes! It's a good job Yowl has courage.'

'Courage!' I think he was lost for words. 'You'd have to be crazy to cl...!'

Diamond raised a lethargic eyebrow. 'Worked, though, didn't it?'

'You clim...?'

I nodded wearily. Now that the adrenaline stuff had deserted my body, I felt like I needed a very long sleep. It wouldn't be easy making it to my windowsill, not with my legs being so stiff.

'How did you get down?' he asked in astonishment.

'I got a lift,' I told him. 'From a friend.'

7

Prisoner

That day, I slept in Diamond's shed, with Shadow curled up next to me keeping me warm. On recent nights, my sleep had been interrupted by thoughts of many things and fears of many others. Maybe I was beginning to put my fears behind me, because I slept as soon as I lay down my head. It was probably just my overwhelming fatigue, but my sleep wasn't disturbed by any dreams or nightmares. I awoke in the late afternoon, desperate to relieve myself. When I tried to move my legs, I cried out in pain.

'What's wrong?' asked an alarmed Shadow.

'Pain!' I gasped.

'Where?'

I took a full inventory of my body. 'Everywhere!' I told her.

'Just lie back,' she purred.

'I can't! I have to go.'

'Oh,' she muttered. 'Come, I'll help you.'

Together we managed to crawl out of the shed. Shadow supported me whenever I threatened to fall. She gave me a limited amount of privacy, but I was completely unable to dig a suitable hole, let alone cover it afterwards. She escorted me back to my home and when I arrived at my cat flap, reluctantly left me. I only had the energy to collapse in my basket. I didn't even notice the tiny creatures jumping around. I closed my eyes and returned to a blissful sleep.

My humans buzzed about, in and out. In response, I could only raise a tired eyelid. Nobody seemed too concerned. Even Lucy didn't seem to notice my distress. I ignored them all and slept until dawn when I was disturbed by a quiet hoot.

My legs were still uncomfortably stiff as I negotiated my way out of my basket. All my muscles screamed for more rest but I knew I had things to do, places to go. I pushed through my cat flap and was greeted by a stationary owl standing alone on the patio. 'Morning Yowl!'

he cried with exaggerated good humour.

'Morning,' I responded miserably, and almost crawled up to him, my body hanging low to the ground.

'Still feeling it, huh?'

'Everything's stiff,' I complained. 'Everything hurts.'

He took a lengthy look at me. 'Here's what I want you to do,' he announced. He then proceeded to take me through a ten minute stretching routine. Everything he asked me to do caused more pain. If there was a part of me I wanted him to leave alone, he honed in on it instinctively. I trusted him and knew that if I completed his exercises, I'd feel a lot better. So I followed his advice as precisely as I could, stretching my muscles further than I'd thought possible. I even gained a couple of spectators, as Diamond and Shadow sat a suitable distance away and watched.

And when I'd finished, I felt a whole lot better. I think much of it was just getting the blood pumping around my body again after such a long period of inactivity.

'Feel better?' he enquired.

'Yes, I do,' I replied, a little confused.

'You have to regain your strength. If you do that routine morning and evening, your muscles will be back to normal in a couple of days.'

I nodded enthusiastically, my neck muscles already feeling smoother. 'I will. Thanks.'

Shadow rushed across and rubbed herself against me. 'How are you feeling, Champ?'

'A little better,' I told her, gently bumping noses.

By this time, Flash had finished her breakfast and heard the commotion. 'Morning all!' she cried, squeezing under the fence. 'Anything new?' she asked, glancing at Hewt.

'Not today,' he said, shaking his head. 'I was out all night and didn't spot anyone acting suspiciously.'

Diamond nodded in acceptance. It was too much to expect a sighting on his first night, but we were all disappointed. Our heads swivelled in response to a short call from the bushes. We were expecting Red, but it was his son Dash, whose nose was visible between the leaves. We all moved up the garden, I more slowly than the others. Even Hewt on his two short legs could move faster than me.

'Uncle Hewt!' Dash screamed in joy, dashing from hiding to join him.

'That can't possibly be Little Dash?' Hewt responded in amazement.

We went through all the greetings once again and Dash promised to convey Hewt's regards to Big Red. Apparently, when they were young, Dash and the other cubs had played for hours with Uncle Hewt and his partner Princess. Bonds formed at that age lasted a lifetime and it was heart-warming to see the two of them together: so totally different, yet so completely relaxed with each other. It just went to show how wrong the accepted stereotype of foxes was.

Ultimately, despite enlisting all the help we could, we were no further forward. We all understood that it would take time. It was just chançe that the foxes would be stalking the same streets as the Tall Man, but Hewt had a far wider range. He could remain aloft and examine multiple streets at the same time. He even had excellent night vision. He remained our best chance.

I struggled through the day feeling useless but knowing there was nothing I could do. Shadow never left my side and I found myself warming to her concern. I slept a lot and each time I awoke, I felt a little better. My body was healing itself slowly. Before I went to sleep that night, I ran through Hewt's exercise routine with Shadow making sure I didn't take it easy.

The next morning, I was almost feeling back to my usual self. My leg muscles still had a hint of dullness, a lingering memory of overuse. Hewt reported that he'd identified a suspicious human, although his hat had been dark green and not black. He'd hovered and watched as the man left food at the junction of two streets. He'd even prepared himself to intervene as the man waited for homeless cats to approach. He'd just watched them eat and moved on to another location, where he repeated his actions.

Apparently, the humans had come to the same conclusion as the animals: feeding homeless cats would ease their hunger and they'd be less likely to approach a dangerous man for food. It made Hewt's job all the more difficult. On the other hand, we hadn't seen any new *Missing* posters. Perhaps he'd ended his reign of terror. Perhaps the danger was over. But deep down, I knew that wasn't the case. Something had interrupted his work. Maybe he'd gone on holiday. Whatever the cause, we were grateful for the respite.

It didn't last long.

Eight days later, *Missing* posters started to appear again and this time they were closer to home. One was stapled to a fence no more than a stone's throw from my front door. It depicted a young tabby by the name of Jess. She'd gone missing from a loving home two days earlier.

So, while we were concentrating on the safety and wellbeing of homeless cats, our perpetrator wasn't discriminating. Jess may have fallen victim to a car, but my money was on the Tall Man. I suppose it boiled down to the fact that cats were greedy. I cast my mind just a few days back to the morning I was introduced to salmon. I'd already had my breakfast, but it didn't stop me lapping up more food when it was available. It was probably our primeval instincts to stock up on food when we could. We didn't know when the next famine was coming. Such subconscious thinking may well have led to the downfall of many cats.

Every morning we'd had a detailed discussion with Hewt. He'd begun his patrols, quite understandably, around the school. As the days went by, he'd widened his search to include the recreation ground, the duck pond and the new housing estate. Every night he chose an area and was vigilant for the entire night, excluding a short period when he had to find food for himself. I think it was the first time in many months that he'd spent so long aloft. He certainly looked exhausted when he appeared every morning. Like Hewt, the foxes were out every night. Their patrols were limited to a street or two, but they never heard or saw anything out of the ordinary.

We needed something to happen.

We needed the Tall Man to make a mistake.

It had always mystified me why there was no noise. If a cat feels threatened, it will usually hiss, growl and finally, screech. A cat's screech can be heard for miles. Yet no-one had reported hearing anything.

We agreed with Hewt to restrict his next night's patrol to our immediate area. We didn't know how the perpetrator operated: whether he opted for different areas every night, or whether when he found an area in which he felt safe, he remained there. We knew he'd been close a few nights' before, so it was as good a guess as any.

I wanted to be up there with Hewt. Every day, I asked him to take me. I knew it would hurt, but at least I'd be doing something. Of course, it was wholly impractical. He was wearing himself out flying all night. He couldn't possibly carry a passenger.

Everyone was tense. We tried to continue the good natured banter as before, but even Ally, the most mild mannered Alsatian imaginable, was on edge. Big Red was rarely seen and Dash and Creeper were always complaining about his foul temper. The only one it didn't seem to affect was Secret. The foxes and dogs were doing everything they possibly could to help, and Hewt was exhausting himself in the search. Digger came by with snippets of information he'd gleaned on his travels, but increasingly, I came to doubt the veracity of a lot of it. He was only passing on gossip and, by its very nature, gossip was unreliable. The pigeons' stories were like social media for animals: anyone could say anything they wanted and there was little or no regard for the truth.

I slept badly throughout the long wait and as a result, I was grumpy during the day. We all wanted to be actively searching for the killer, but we knew that Hewt and the foxes were our best chance. Shadow and I had become almost inseparable and she had grown used to my moods. Diamond's humans had seen so much of her that they'd virtually adopted her. She hadn't got a bed inside the warm house, but they'd provided blankets for her in the shed and ensured she was well fed every day. It was the same gourmet food that Diamond enjoyed, so I frequently helped finish it off. She wasn't doing badly for a homeless cat who was, to the best of our knowledge, the Tall Man's only surviving victim.

Occasionally I saw stories in the local paper about the Croydon Cat Killer. Residents were still asking questions and, in the face of growing police apathy, demanding answers. The police were issuing statements in an attempt to placate the bereaved: *We are doing everything within our power to ensure that the perpetrator is brought to justice.* And so it went on. It's important to emphasise that, at that point, there appeared no doubt that they accepted that there was a cat killer on the loose. While they were having no luck finding him, they weren't denying his existence.

Then one evening I was snoozing on Jo's lap, long after Lucy had gone to bed. My eyelids were drooping, but I was still alert. It was after dark and you never knew when the call might come. They were watching television: the news. It all sounded very serious and it seemed like nothing good ever happened. They should call it the Bad News. Maybe there wasn't any good news. My eyes opened wide when I saw the headline of their next story at the bottom of the screen: *In Croydon, police are hunting a man believed to be responsible for the deaths of over one hundred cats.* I immediately tensed and was riveted to the screen. They had a reporter on the streets of Croydon but I didn't recognise the location. *On a quiet road beside the swimming pool, Arthur became the Cat Killer's latest victim.* I could feel my hackles rising, my tail plumping up.

'Aah!' screamed Jo and I was catapulted up in the air. When I landed smoothly on my feet, my tail was rigid and I was ready for anything. 'You hurt me!' she went on.

I looked at her leg, currently clothed in thin, pale blue pyjamas. There were four pinpricks of blood visible. I hadn't realised I'd been that tense. I mumbled a quick apology. I certainly hadn't meant to hurt her.

'I think we ought to make sure Yowl stays in at nights,' Brian commented.

'Yes, we can lock the cat flap.'

'Just until this maniac is caught.'

What!

That wouldn't do! Where would I be when I heard Hewt's cry if I was trapped inside the house? I had to be able to join the hunt. I yowled pathetically in an attempt to win some sympathy. 'Don't worry,' he went on, talking to me. 'It won't be for long.'

They were serious!

They were going to imprison me in the house overnight!

There could be all manner of unfortunate consequences. I couldn't allow it to happen but they sounded deadly serious. How could I prevent it?

The first night I searched frantically for a way out. The kitchen windows had those lever-type locks. If you pressed hard enough from below, the arm came free of the two pins that held it in place. Then you could push it open. They were just too stiff. I tried and I tried but my little arms were too weak. I didn't have opposable thumbs, a feature of which I'd become aware in Lucy's latest animal book. They would have helped. I just couldn't do it. I had to find another way.

The second night, I had a brainwave. The litter tray had long since been dispensed with and to date, I hadn't had a single accident. I waited until everyone was asleep, then I squatted in the middle of the kitchen and left them a very smelly message. The sort of message that I usually dug a hole in the flower beds to conceal.

I had to stay in the room for the rest of the night, which wasn't pleasant, but their reaction in the morning was suitably horrified. Jo cleaned it up and Brian actually suggested, 'Do we still have the litter tray?'

Fortunately, the answer was no. It wasn't one of those things that you kept around the house to remind you of your pet's youth. 'He probably won't do it again,' he remarked.

I jumped off the windowsill in a flash. My legs were a bit sleepy, but I made it to the middle of the room and began to squat. 'No!' the female cried and threw open the back door.

Success!

That night, they gave me strict orders not to leave the garden. It was dangerous out there. I nodded gravely. I knew the dangers only too well and had no intention of leaving the garden unless Hewt gave the signal. Then it would be teamwork: dog, foxes, cats, squirrel and an owl would come together as one in the face of adversity. We'd protect each other. What hope had a mere human against such a band of animal brothers and sisters?

8

Positive ID & a Close Encounter

Three nights later, I heard the call. An owl's hoot could travel for miles and we were all ready. My sleep had been light since we'd all been on standby. My eyes sprang open and I almost fell off the windowsill in my haste. I leapt through the cat flap in a single movement, racing next door to the agreed assembly point, outside Flash's back door. Secret was already there, his nose twitching frantically. He'd clearly woken Flash, who was stumbling through her cat flap as though still half asleep.

'Geronimo!' came a cry from the end of the garden.

We looked round and there was Ginger careering through the flowerbed and chasing down the lawn, closely followed by Shadow. They joined us in the circle and we all looked at each other. The foxes would already be out, hopefully reacting to Hewt's cry, and we weren't expecting Diamond to join us. 'Let's go,' I whispered.

'Where?' asked Ginger.

'The street,' I told him. I wasn't sure where Hewt's cry had come from and I wanted to wait until I heard another before committing myself. We travelled silently down the passage between the houses and stopped on the pavement. We all listened intently, but heard precisely nothing. A few distant cars were audible, but there was a distinct lack of owl's cries. I'd have to have a word with him. A single cry was not enough to pinpoint his location. There was a definite flaw in our strategy.

Then we heard him again. It sounded like the cry was coming from some distance, and considerably weaker than before, but we all agreed on the direction. We headed off as fast as we could, making sure we stayed together at all times. It meant travelling quite slowly, because Flash was old and incapable of sprinting. I wasn't sure how she'd react if she came face to face with the Tall Man. I'd make it my business to ensure she stayed clear of any danger. Hewt called out every few minutes, leading us in the right direction.

We ended up in a deserted street with little in the way of lighting. Hewt was propped up against a scarlet pillar box, his head drooping. 'What happened? Are you alright?' I asked urgently.

'Just a little...' he stammered. 'Hit my head... Be alright in a minute.'

'What happened?' Flash repeated.

He took a deep breath and accepted Secret's offer of his back to lean on and continued in quick staccato sentences. 'He was here,' he started. 'There was a cat...' He hesitated. 'Hadn't seen him before. He was eating. He tried to pick him up. Saw something in his other hand.' He tried to stand on his own two feet and succeeded, wobbling slightly. 'Had to stop him. Flew at his head. I was going for his eyes.' He took a deep breath. 'He flapped at me with his arm.' He stopped abruptly, looking confused.

'He tried to kill you!' Ginger screamed.

'No. No, he didn't,' Hewt insisted. Now we were all confused. 'He caught me with his arm,' he explained. 'Not the one with the knife. The other arm.'

'And?' Flash urged.

'I hit my head on the pillar box. Couldn't fly. Dizzy.'

That would explain the length of time between his first call and his second, while we were waiting to determine the direction. 'You're lucky he didn't go for you when you were on the ground,' I told him.

'Funny thing,' he muttered. 'I thought he was going to but he came over and helped me back to my feet. He said something too,' he recalled.

'What did he say?' I asked.

'He said, "Beautiful creature. I would never hurt you."'

That was strange. Maybe he limited his victims to cats and foxes. I thought back to what I'd been told about Snort's injury. The Tall Man hadn't initially targeted him. He'd only struck out when attacked. Snort had his arm in his mouth. That must have hurt. The more I thought about it, the more I convinced myself that he'd acted in desperation. He was only interested in targeting cats.

'What happened then?' Flash asked.

'Dash and Creeper arrived. He heard them coming and took off.'

He'd had a narrow escape. 'Where did they go?'

'They followed him. Hopefully they'll find out where he lives,' he told us. It was clear that his dazed state was only temporary. He was already getting back to normal.

He'd saved the life of another cat, but risked his own. I didn't want any of us getting hurt. It was some time before Hewt declared himself fit enough to fly. We stayed with him to ensure he was safe. It was a miserable small street corner: no cars passed and no pedestrians walked our way. When Hewt was back in the air, we returned to Flash's garden. We'd have to wait for the foxes to return. We had no idea how far they'd have to travel, or whether they'd be able to keep up with him. Hewt had been too disorientated to notice how he'd made his getaway. If he had a car parked nearby, it would be too quick even for the foxes.

We sat around uneasily. It was the darkest part of the night, the early hours, when all decent animals were asleep in bed. We were all anxious, but Flash still managed to fall asleep as soon as she took to her basket. Ginger suggested we let Diamond know what was going on, but he hadn't appeared. We decided to let him sleep. Ginger, Shadow and I tried to talk about things, but we really hadn't the appetite. We were all too tense, waiting for news.

We didn't have to wait too long. After about half an hour, three wet noses appeared at the end of the garden: Dash, Creeper and Red. We chased up the lawn and screeched to a stop facing them. 'What happened?' I asked.

Creeper took up the story. 'We followed him home. He was on a bicycle, so we had to race to keep up. We can show you his house.'

'That's great!' cried Shadow. 'Is it far?'

'Just the other side of the recreation ground,' she was told.

'Well done getting to Hewt,' I praised the pair.

'We were waiting for another call. We weren't certain where he was,' Dash explained.

I nodded. 'We were waiting too.'

'We were lucky tonight,' Red added with a

note of caution. 'But the boys did well.'

We all agreed enthusiastically. 'We're going to have a rest,' Dash told us. 'If you're here early in the morning, we'll show you where he lives.'

'We'll be here,' I assured him.

Thanks to the bravery of the foxes, we'd identified the Tall Man and found out where he lived. Now we just needed to figure out what to do. I was working on some 'punishments' I considered appropriate. They just needed a little fine tuning. There were rather a lot of problems with them. I needed to talk them through with the others. They'd find a way to make them work. We were ready to take the initiative, ready to hit back, hard.

'I have an idea,' I announced to an excited gathering the following morning. We were all up early and waiting for the foxes to put in an appearance.

'What is it?' asked Diamond. We'd brought him up to date with the night's momentous events and, although he was urging caution in the face of Hewt's injuries, he was raring to go.

'In our house, we have a magic fire stick,' I told them. 'It makes fire!'

'Why?'

'They use it to light the gas on the cooker.'

'What do you plan to do with it?' asked a puzzled Flash.

'I thought we could all get together and get into his house. Then we could build up a pile of dry leaves and sticks under some furniture or the curtains. Then we could set fire to it with the fire stick.' I sat back. I was feeling pretty proud of myself, I can tell you.

'The house would be empty, right?' asked Flash cautiously.

'Er... Yes! We could keep watch and strike while it was empty.'

After some moments' silent reflection, Flash and Diamond exchanged a telling glance. Diamond looked up at me. 'You seriously want to set fire to his house?' he asked sternly.

'That's the plan.'

He shook his head sadly. 'There's a word for that,' he told us.

'Justice!' Secret suggested excitedly.

'No, arson. That's what it is. And it's illegal.'

'So's killing cats,' Secret persisted.

'Two wrongs do not make a right.'

There was a tense silence.

'How would we get inside the house?' Flash asked.

I *had* considered that problem, but hadn't yet identified a suitable solution. 'We're cats!' I reminded her. 'We'll find a way.'

'Can you even use this fire stick?' Diamond asked. The pair of them were successfully identifying all the weak points in my plan.

'Well, no,' I replied. 'I don't have opposable thumbs.'

Flash looked even more puzzled. 'What are they?'

'Like humans. They can touch all their fingers with their thumbs.'

'I used to know a cat like that,' Diamond told us. 'Mittens, we used to call her.'

'I remember her,' Flash confirmed. 'She fell out of a tree, didn't she?'

He nodded sadly. 'They couldn't save her.'

We followed the familiar pattern of taking a minute to lower our heads and remember departed friends. Then Flash asked, 'How will you make the fire stick work, then?'

'It has a button on the side. If we lay it down on the floor, someone heavy could stand on the button and make fire,' I told them.

It took a moment.

'Why's everyone looking at me?' Diamond enquired.

'You could do it,' I assured him.

'Listen, Junior. I think Diamond's days of breaking into houses and setting them on fire are over, don't you?' Flash scolded.

I had to nod in agreement. I knew that if we asked, Diamond would do his best, but he was just too old, not mobile enough to help. 'Ally said he'll help,' Ginger chipped in.

That was significant. Ally had the weight to light the fire stick. Unfortunately, he also had sufficient bulk to ensure that entry to the house could be a problem. He wasn't flexible like the cats and squirrels. However, there was no-one I'd rather have protecting me if it came to a fight. An Alsatian could take down a human, no problem.

'When do you plan to do this?' asked Diamond.

There was a general silence. 'We need to study his movements,' I told him.

'Why?' he asked, not unreasonably.

'To find out the best time to strike.'

Diamond nodded. 'Just watching, alright? Don't do anything... impulsive,' he warned me.

'Surveillance is a good idea,' Ginger agreed. 'We'll need the foxes again for nights.'

Diamond stomped away, clearly unhappy.

We arranged a rota to cover the daytime. Flash and I would take the mornings, with Shadow and Ginger the afternoons. It was too dangerous for anyone to keep watch alone. We'd also alert Ally, Hewt and the foxes, who'd be listening for any signs of distress. Personally, I thought it more likely Hewt and the foxes would be asleep, but Ally might hear our cries. He could then raise the alarm closer to home. It was the best we could do.

The foxes finally arrived, rather later than anticipated. They explained that all the nights spent on surveillance had seriously affected their food supplies. They'd had to spend a couple of extra hours foraging to ensure their families had enough food. Where on earth they found enough tasty morsels remained a mystery, but I'd gathered that a fox was none too particular when it came to eating. No bins in the area were safe on rubbish collection day. Humans threw away an awful lot of very good, edible food.

Dash and Creeper led the way. We all trailed behind. The initial excitement had decreased somewhat after our lengthy wait. We just wanted to identify the house, search for suitable openings, and plot our revenge. We avoided the main roads and kept to the minor lanes and pathways. On a couple of occasions we had to skirt human pedestrians, but we managed to do so without making significant detours. It was a long walk! We passed the school, the swimming baths and crossed the recreation ground. We watched as several trains sped past on the railway line that ran parallel to the road. Then we took a turn down a short street that ended abruptly at the railway embankment. There were only four houses on each side.

I stopped on the corner. So did everyone

else, except the foxes. My heart was beating fast. I felt like Daniel about to enter the lions' den. I wished I hadn't spent so long reading *The Children's Bible* with Lucy for her Religion lesson. I tried to give Flash a reassuring smile but my face muscles weren't working. The foxes had stopped beside the road, wondering where we'd gone. I took a deep breath and crept along the pavement, keeping as low as I could.

We joined the foxes opposite number 23 Railway Cuttings. 'That's the one,' Creeper told us. I nipped behind a short brick wall fronting the garden opposite. Each house was set back from the road behind a pocket handkerchief front lawn and a gravel driveway for parking a car. Reluctantly, I peered over the top of the wall. Number 23 had no car present, but I could see the pathway continue to the rear. There was a gate but it didn't reach the ground. There would be sufficient space for us all to pass underneath, even Ally.

In the front garden were several bushes that could be used for shelter, if we wanted to get that close. Several single tracks were visible in the gravel driveway, evidence that he cycled regularly. We didn't know if he had a job. Presumably, if he was out most nights, he would be asleep in the mornings.

We had to keep watch on his movements and discover whether anyone else lived in the house. If he had a family, that would complicate matters. Somehow I didn't associate the Tall Man with a wife and children. That didn't mean he lived alone, of course. If we managed to watch his house for a few days, or weeks, everything would become clear. Most importantly, we had to remain unobserved.

Dash strolled quite casually across the pavement. 'You can hide in the bushes in the front garden,' he told us. 'They're quite thick. He won't see you.'

I looked at Flash. She didn't appear keen to move. 'Ready?' I asked.

'Um...'

'Don't worry,' I assured her. 'We can outrun a human.'

'*You* can,' she replied.

'I'll look after you.'

'Come on,' Dash called. 'We'll come with

you.'

Apprehensively, we trailed behind the foxes and skulked into the front garden, not daring to get too close to the house. I could already detect a horrible scent. It was exactly what I was expecting from such a monster.

'In here,' Creeper suggested, pointing his nose under a canopy of bushes.

Flash and I crept into a suitable position, from where we could observe the house. Hopefully, we were sufficiently concealed. The others departed very quickly and left us to it. Ginger and Shadow would be back in the afternoon to relieve us.

Everything was quiet. Despite her fears, Flash soon found a comfortable place and curled up, closing her eyes. 'You take first watch, kid,' she whispered. 'Wake me up in an hour.' Within a few minutes, she was snoring contentedly.

I watched the windows for any sign of movement. I kept half an eye on the gate in case it sprang open. I couldn't see a bicycle, so presumably it was at the back of the house. I could hear all sorts of noises: birds cheeping, insects wandering and worms tunnelling. I tried climbing a nearby bush to get a better view. Ow! It had spikes. I decided to stay on the ground.

Within minutes, I was bored. My eyelids began to flutter closed. That wouldn't do! I considered myself more as a sentry than a lookout. I had to stay alert. I was just considering the best route to take a look around the back when the gate flew open. I ducked down lower and nudged Flash. She turned over and went back to sleep. This was serious. Hewt and the foxes had worked tirelessly to get us to this stage. We had to be professional.

I watched with my mouth wide open as the Tall Man came into view pushing a bicycle. His scent preceded him: an unpleasant, unclean odour. I cowered down as I watched him come towards us. The gravel crunched under his feet. He was tall and ugly, with a long nose and hooded eyelids. There was a grey pallor to his skin, like he never saw the sun. His eyes were cruel, brown and unfeeling. He was wearing blue jeans and a black leather jacket. His hair was covered by a black woollen cap.

I tried nudging Flash again, but she was deeply asleep. He came towards us, throwing his leg over the crossbar and riding out onto the road. I wasn't a fox. Although I could run very fast over short distances, there was no way I could keep up with a bicycle.

With the Tall Man out of the way, it might be safe to take a look around. I put my nose in the air and sniffed. I couldn't detect any other human scents. I was aware that he might have a family. He might even be a lodger, sharing the house with someone else. There was so much we had to learn before we could make a move.

I checked Flash. She was still asleep. I'd been presented with a chance to explore without any danger of being seen by the Tall Man. The crunch of the gravel would give me advance warning should he return. Flash would no doubt remind me that our job was merely to observe and report back. I wanted more.

Cautiously, I left the shelter of the bushes and crept along the flowerbed. I didn't want to take to the gravel. It would make noise. I looked all around me and hopped up onto the front room's windowsill. Everything was quiet inside. I couldn't see any movement. The room was papered in a dark floral pattern. The furniture was dark wood: the kind everyone said was out of fashion now. Two armchairs and a two-seater sofa cast a semi-circle around an old fashioned television.

Suddenly, there was a piercing shriek.

Like a shot, I jumped down and hightailed it back to the bushes. Flash still hadn't moved a muscle. I sat there and tried to control my breathing. That was scary! I attempted to recall the shriek. It definitely wasn't human. It was something from the animal kingdom. What would be sharing his front room if it wasn't a cat or a dog? I envisaged all manner of creatures, conjuring them straight from the pages of Lucy's *The World's Greatest Predators* book. When it became apparent that whatever it was, it wasn't coming after me, I grew braver. I checked for any activity on the street. It was silent. I returned to the windowsill.

At the rear of the room I could see a cage hanging from a stand. Inside was a huge grey parrot. I knew from books that they had a loud cry. I looked at its talons. They looked vicious. I wouldn't like to meet it on a dark night. Involuntarily, my back tensed where Hewt's claws had broken the skin. The wounds were still tender.

I jumped down, having learned nothing of note: nothing except that our target was a parrot lover. I scooted along the front of the house. I knew I shouldn't but, ignoring Diamond's advice, I dipped under the gate. I wanted to discover as much as I could before the Tall Man returned. The path continued past the house and all the way up the garden. I followed it, sniffing for any sign of danger.

The moment I stepped past the house, there was chaos: loud squawking, screeching and fluttering. I crouched down in preparation for an attack. Nothing happened but the noise persisted. This wasn't the twitter of small birds, the quacking of ducks, or even the clucking of chickens. This was the incessant shrieking of large birds, raptors, birds of prey. I took a look to my left and a huge, wood-framed aviary came into view. I didn't want to get too close but I could see kestrels, kites and buzzards.

I wished I had Lucy's *i-SPY Birds* book with me. I could have ticked off several hard-to-find species.

I was trying to count the number of birds, when I heard, 'Silence!'

I looked around for the speaker but couldn't identify it. The noise continued at deafening levels.

'Silence!' he commanded again.

This time, the noise began to die down. A huge, red kite fluttered and landed on a branch near the front of the cage. 'Who are you?' he demanded with a flap of his wings.

His wingspan was nearly as big as a human. I could only stare at him, hoping the wire mesh was secure.

'What are you doing here?' he went on, his hooked beak quivering in indignation.

The massive cage stretched halfway down the back garden. It was stuffed with raptors. The smallest was considerably bigger than me. The largest would have given Ally a run for his money. I stood there spellbound, trying to identify all the species.

'Do you have authorisation to be in this

sector?' he asked aggressively.

'Auth...'

'I believe he's an intruder,' a peregrine falcon suggested.

He was quite lovely. His markings were exquisite. 'What?' I stuttered.

'You shouldn't be here,' I was told sternly.

'Neither should you,' I replied, attending to an itch on my hind leg. 'You should be free.'

They all turned and stared at me. 'Free?'

'You should be flying over mountains and valleys, catching small rodents to eat,' I explained.

'Small rodents! Have you taken leave of your senses?'

It was my turn to stare. 'Are you an osprey?'

'I am,' she replied. 'And I'm perfectly happy with the food I receive here, thank you very much.'

I took a step closer to get a better look. I knew that they'd been considered extinct in the UK until recently. Immediately, there was a mass fluttering, trying to keep their distance. I didn't think they had anything to worry about. Any one of them could have picked me up and carried me away for dinner.

I took a couple of steps back, trying to lessen their anxiety, but not before scratching a very persistent itch under my chin. I was standing on the fringe of the lawn when I heard the sound of gravel crunching. The Tall Man was returning. He couldn't find me there! I'd become another statistic. I should have listened to Diamond. I should have stayed with Flash. Frantically, I looked around for somewhere to hide. There were no bushes, no sheds, and no trees. I heard the gate being pushed open. My time had run out. All I could do was take a flying leap into a nearby wheelbarrow. It wasn't very deep. I had to crouch down to remain unobserved.

I heard a metallic object being propped against the wall, presumably his bicycle. He noticed the birds' agitated state straight away. He started to coo, attempting to calm them. 'What's got you so excited?' he asked. 'Not another cat!'

I took a peek above the edge, keeping my ears uncomfortably flat. He was examining the ground beside the aviary. He picked something up in his fingers. It appeared to be a few hairs from my luxurious coat. 'I'll get you!' he shouted, withdrawing something from his jacket pocket. It was silver and looked like a pen: the murder weapon! He continued to scream, 'I'll get you! I'll skin you! I'll use your bones for toothpicks!'

I could hear his footsteps drawing closer. I never thought I'd be this close to the Tall Man. I cowered down in the wheelbarrow, shaking uncontrollably. I hoped he wouldn't see me. Suddenly, it got darker. He was standing between me and the sun. I tried to make myself even smaller. I could see the top of his hat! He was coming straight for me.

'Meyooow!' came a very welcome cry from the front garden. It was Flash. 'Meyooow!'

'You blasted...!' he shouted before running towards the gate. I heard him pull it open. I hoped Flash was a safe distance away.

I jumped out of the wheelbarrow, shot across the flowerbed and leapt over the wooden fence on the other side of the garden. I'd just smelled something that made my fur rise, when I landed gracefully about four feet from a sleeping Rottweiler. I stood very still as I watched his drooping eyes slowly open. We looked at each other for a fraction of a second. Then he was chasing me. I made for the gate to the front of the property. No good! It was cat and dog-proof. It almost reached the ground. To turn around would have invited death between a Rottweiler's jaws. I leapt as high as I could and, using an adjacent fig tree as a springboard, landed on top of the gate. I took a breath and gave him an expression meant to convey the superiority of the feline species. He charged the gate, making it shake violently. My feet slipped. I clung on desperately with my claws and dragged myself back upright. He continued to jump up at me, but I was high enough, just. Exhausted, I leapt down into the front driveway.

I crept back to the pavement and looked for any sign of danger. The Tall Man was nowhere in sight. Hopefully he was attending to his birds. I couldn't see Flash. I let loose a quiet yowl. I didn't want to attract his attention again. An unconcerned Flash wandered from the end of the street. 'Hey, kid,' she greeted me with a smile. She didn't look like she had a hair out of place.

'Hey,' I responded. We bumped noses. 'Thanks for your help.'

'My pleasure! He woke me up when he came back,' she told me. 'Couldn't find you. Figured you must be round the back.'

I nodded and filled her in on what I'd discovered.

'Bird lover, huh?' she pondered.

'They're beautiful,' I told her. 'So big!' I went on to explain what lay in wait in the next garden along.

She chuckled. 'Rottweilers! They sure are dumb!'

I thought we'd probably had enough excitement for one morning. Instead of waiting for Ginger and Shadow, we made our way home. I was beginning to understand the layout of my home town. I wasn't confident that I could find my way back home on my own yet, but I was learning. The smells were all familiar, including some seriously unpleasant ones left by my fellow males.

Diamond was lounging in the sun when we

made it to his garden. Ginger was nowhere to be seen. He shook his head sadly after I explained the morning's events. 'Humans say we have nine lives,' he told me. 'I think you've just used up another two.'

'Eek!'

'You have to learn patience. Your job was to observe from a safe place,' he told me. 'Instead, you went exploring and nearly got yourself killed.' I dropped my head. I knew he was right. I was too impetuous. 'If Flash hadn't saved your skin, you'd have been another victim.'

We all lowered our heads. It's like we were all synchronised.

'However,' he went on, 'you did obtain some useful intelligence.'

'Mmm,' purred Flash in agreement, licking her bottom.

'We now know he's a bird-lover who has an irrational hatred of cats.'

'It's not like we catch many birds,' I muttered.

'You might not, Junior,' Flash commented. She looked at Diamond. 'Remember Lightning?'

He blew out his cheeks. 'He was fast! They never saw him coming.'

'Two, three every day,' Flash added. 'Sparrows stopped coming to his garden.'

'Couldn't outrun that car though,' Flash muttered. Once again, they lowered their heads in memory of a lost friend.

'You know,' I started after a suitable pause. 'When the Tall Man was in the papers, my humans locked me in at night. I hated it!' They both nodded in agreement but didn't seem to get my point. 'Don't birds hate being kept in a cage?'

They looked at each other. 'From what you've told me, I suspect that they were probably hatched in captivity. There's no trade in ospreys, for example. They're too rare. There *is* a trade in stolen eggs, so I've been told.'

'What difference does that make?' I asked.

'When an animal's been in a cage for its entire life,' Flash explained, 'it doesn't know what freedom is.'

'You don't miss what you've never had,' Diamond added. 'They've never flown over hills and valleys.'

'They've never been taught how to catch their own food,' Flash continued.

'Mind you, they'd probably figure it out when they got hungry,' Diamond added.

'I don't know,' Flash said with a shake of her head. 'Birds aren't known for their intelligence. Have you tried talking to a sparrow?'

'I've never got close enough,' I admitted.

'All they ever think about is food and nests.' Diamond nodded in confirmation. 'Look at Digger. He's good company, but he has no concept of time and his memory is appalling. He can't remember what happened the previous day. Do you have goldfish in your house?'

'No.'

'I once spent a whole morning trying to get our goldfish to remember my name. He had quite a good size bowl. I sat there watching him. When he swam past he said, *Hello, what's your name*? I told him and he swam off. Ten seconds later, he'd be round again saying, *Hello, what's your name*? It was hopeless.'

We pondered that for a few seconds before Flash asked, 'Why are we talking about goldfish?'

Diamond looked confused. 'I don't remember.' They both had a good chuckle. 'Getting old, you know.'

'Ain't that the truth?' Flash confirmed.

'Can we get back to birds in cages?' I asked.

'Oh, yes! It's like this,' he explained. 'Some birds are quite happy in cages. I don't think they know they're supposed to be free.'

'Except parrots,' Flash suggested.

'Oh, parrots! Don't get me started.' He shook his head. 'Exceptionally devious creatures.'

'Devious?' I asked.

'Never trust a parrot!' He instructed sternly.

'He had a parrot,' I reminded them.

'Don't expect any help from him.'

I was surprised. I thought animals stuck together. We all smelled Ginger before he appeared. I think my sense of smell was improving. 'Wassup Dudes?' he cried. Shadow followed in his wake.

We had to run through the morning's events again for their benefit. There was a sharp intake of breath from Shadow when I recounted my meeting with the Rottweiler. 'I don't like it,' Ginger admitted. 'It's dangerous.'

'Not if you stay hidden,' Diamond told him sternly. By now, we all knew that Ginger would attempt to get out of doing anything with even a hint of danger.

'Don't worry,' Shadow purred. 'I'll look after you.'

Reluctantly, she dragged him off in the direction of Railway Cuttings. They'd keep a watch for the afternoon and report back later. Flash lay down next to Diamond and they slowly fell asleep. I returned home and dozed on the windowsill.

9

Surveillance & Scapegoats

I awoke when Lucy returned home from school. I felt I'd been neglecting her of late, so I gave her my full attention. I was rewarded with a handful of fish biscuits. I went upstairs with her and prepared for an afternoon's reading. I was disappointed when she pulled out a book on the solar system. It was a bit simplistic for me and failed to mention the hypothetical Planet Nine I'd learned about in the newspaper.

I hopped off and headed for Diamond's garden. They were all assembled, Diamond, Flash, Ginger and Shadow. 'What happened?' I asked. They should still be observing our target.

'Ginger got cold paws,' Shadow explained, shaking her head sadly.

'It's dangerous!' he cried.

'What happened?'

'He went out just after we got there,' she told me. 'Came back an hour later with a huge box balanced on his handlebars. Then he spent the afternoon up a ladder fixing cameras to the front wall.'

'Cameras?'

'Strange things!' she informed me. 'They have little eyes all around the lens.'

'Sounds like infrared cameras,' I suggested.

'What are they?' Shadow asked.

'Um...' I wasn't too sure.

'And cute little boxes with red lights.'

'Motion detectors.' I was glad I'd spent some time studying a home security brochure when it had been pushed through the letterbox. 'That makes life more difficult.'

'I don't think he has a job,' Shadow suggested.

'Hmm.' We needed to think about this. Our plans would have to change accordingly. We didn't want to be observed. They could even be heat sensitive.

'Did anyone see *The Birdman of Alcatraz*?' Diamond asked. Nobody had. 'Great film!'

I failed to see the relevance. 'What about it?'

'Just thinking,' he mumbled. 'Our man is a bit like the Birdman of Croydon.'

'Did the Alcatraz birdman hate cats?' I asked.

'Well, no, but he was in prison.'

'What for?'

'I can't remember.'

I opened and closed my mouth several times like a goldfish. He chuckled to himself. 'You'll be old one day, youngster!'

'We need to take some action,' I implored.

Shadow looked ready but Ginger went pale. Flash and Diamond just shook their heads. 'This is day one, kid,' Diamond drawled. 'We agreed to observe his movements, find a pattern, and decide the best time to strike.'

'Well, yes,' I admitted.

'What are you planning to do?' Flash asked. 'Because the more I think about it, the more uncomfortable I am with burning his house down.'

'Err.'

'He'd have to move,' Shadow pointed out.

'He'd just start up somewhere else,' Diamond told her. 'We want to eliminate the problem, not move it into someone else's back garden.'

I knew they were right, but I couldn't shake the feeling that we needed to strike back hard.

'And what about the birds?' Flash asked. 'If the house catches fire, the birds could all die. They're innocent. They're not killing cats.'

I thought about that. 'I think the aviary is too far away.'

'What about the parrot?' she added.

I had no answer to that. If the house caught fire, the parrot would perish.

'We could open his bird cages, let all the birds free,' Shadow suggested.

We looked at each other. They hadn't seen the birds. They were dangerous carnivores. No-one would be safe. However, it was a plan that would hurt him. 'Did you see how the cages are secured?' Flash enquired.

I hadn't had time to look. 'No,' I muttered.

'Besides,' Diamond added, 'that would make him very angry. He'd probably escalate his attacks.'

'Especially if his cameras record a bunch of cats coming through his front garden,' Flash stated sombrely.

'It's a clowder of cats,' I mumbled.

'What?'

'The collective noun for cats: it's a clowder.'

'I've never heard that before in my life,' Diamond admitted.

'Unless they're wild cats,' I continued, 'then it's a destruction.'

'Destruction!' Shadow exclaimed. 'How do you know?'

'Lucy has a book of collective nouns. It took her a very long time to learn them all.'

'I stand corrected,' Flash said. 'Especially if he records a clowder of cats in his front garden.'

I nodded mutely. She was right.

'So what do we do?' I asked.

'I've been thinking,' Diamond informed us. 'I have a friend, Cotton. I sleep in her shed sometimes.' Flash gave him a dirty look. 'Her human is a policeman. Maybe he could help.'

Flash looked at me enquiringly. 'Can you write?'

Gulp! 'I can't hold a pencil.'

'If we could get a message to the policeman, we could tell him where the Tall Man lives.'

I wasn't so sure. 'We need to catch him in the act.'

In the morning, we met up with the foxes from the night patrol. 'All quiet,' they told us. 'I've never been so bored in my life.'

'Did you take a look around?' I asked.

'Certainly not! Our instructions were to remain out of sight and observe.'

Diamond nodded firmly. 'Good job lads. See you tomorrow.' They departed slowly. Diamond turned to me and chided, 'Remain hidden and observe! If only we'd told *you* that.'

I wasn't impressed. It was my turn on watch. Flash dragged herself after me. She was no spring chicken and didn't seem to have a sprint in her. What she was missing in speed, she made up for in smarts. Her years of experience made me feel invincible when I was with her. She'd already saved my skin once, I didn't believe she'd ever let anything bad happen to me. I looked upon her as my substitute mother.

We saw for ourselves the new security cameras he'd installed, together with the red lights that came on when you moved. Actually, they came on when anything moved. A light breeze disturbing the bushes produced a flashing response that wouldn't have looked out of place in an amusement arcade. I counted six of them, covering every direction. Special attention was given to the gate that led to the back garden. There was absolutely no chance of getting through unobserved, unless we could approach from the back.

While Flash gently dozed, I checked close to the ground for lasers or infrared motion detectors. I even cast my eyes towards the roof. I wouldn't have been surprised to see defence drones emerging from the gables. He'd managed to accumulate a very impressive collection of some of Britain's rarest birds. He wasn't taking any chances over their security. I decided that it was too dangerous to investigate through the gate and merely observed.

*

On the fourth day of our 24-hour surveillance, I received a most unpleasant surprise. As usual, I was first to the local paper when it fell on the mat. For some reason, it took an unusually long time to flip it so I could see the front page. I couldn't believe the headline: *Croydon Cat Killer Finally Unmasked.* Initially, my spirits leapt. Presumably, they'd identified him and arrested him.

As I read on, my heart dropped. The police had closed the case after post mortems on twenty-five dead cats. Their conclusion was that they'd died from blunt force trauma, or incidents with cars. They believed their bodies had been mauled after death by predators. Although it didn't specify, the finger was firmly pointed in the direction of foxes. Despite the anger and disbelief of local residents, the police would be taking no further action.

I thought long and hard about what I'd read in the local paper. It was all wrong. Although some cats may well have fallen foul of cars, I knew the foxes wouldn't maul their remains. It was especially cruel knowing that they were out every night keeping watch on the real killer. Without their help, we would never have identified him. Now cats in the neighbourhood were safe thanks to Creeper and Dash's patrols.

I wandered in a daze under the fence and looked for Flash. She was enjoying the evening sunshine laid out in a most undignified manner. 'Flash!' I hissed. 'We've got problems.'

She opened her drooping eyes and licked her lips. 'What's up, Junior?'

'I've just read the local paper,' I told her breathlessly. 'The police have closed the case.'

'Great!' she cried. 'They've got him!'

'No. They say there's no evidence that a human was involved.' She looked puzzled, so I went on. 'They think the cats died in car accidents and were then attacked by predators. They think it was the foxes!' I shrieked.

She raised her eyes to the heavens. 'Par for the course,' she mumbled.

'What?' I didn't understand how golf was involved.

'The police hate unsolved crimes,' she explained patiently. 'They've been looking for this guy for years. It's bad for their crime statistics.'

I shook my head. I still didn't understand.

She took a deep breath. 'When they can't find the real culprit, they pretend that there wasn't a crime in the first place. Either that or when they catch a small-time villain, they charge him with lots of other crimes. It gets them off the books, you see. Increases their clear-up rate.'

'That's unfair!'

'That's humans!'

'We should tell Red,' I urged.

'I suppose.' She didn't sound enthusiastic. Maybe it was just that she would rather be asleep. She'd already been up several hours during the day. She must have been exhausted.

It was still early evening, but I thought the foxes might be up preparing for the night shift. We wandered towards their lair. Flash dragged herself several paces behind me. When we approached the foxes' territory, the sentries bowed their heads and let us pass. I sat down in the customary waiting area and wondered where Flash had disappeared to. Glancing behind, I saw her shamelessly flirting with one of the sentries. 'Flash!' I called.

She reluctantly tore herself away and joined me, stifling a yawn. We heard him before we saw him: heavy footsteps gradually drawing closer. Several members of his family joined us in a circle. They were all aware of the situation. They knew that we were all striving night and day to help catch the killer. Everyone wanted to hear the latest news.

Red sat down opposite us and stared at Flash. 'You're looking lovely this evening, my dear,' he purred.

'Oh! Thank you, Red.' She yawned loudly. 'I just woke up.'

I cleared my throat loudly.

'Yes, Junior?'

'I thought I ought to tell you, the police have closed the cat killer case,' I explained.

'They caught him?' he asked doubtfully.

'No.' I took a pause. 'They think the cats were hit by cars and mauled by predators.'

'Typical!' he cried loudly. 'I suppose they're blaming us?'

I swallowed loudly. 'Yes,' I muttered.

'It's great, isn't it? Anything that goes

wrong, it's always the foxes' fault!'

I didn't know what to add. I didn't want to make him any more angry.

'Look at that farmer last week,' he went on to illustrate his point. 'Someone attacks her chickens. They just assume it must have been foxes!'

I hadn't heard about that, but I noticed several foxes' focus on Dash. He looked up guiltily. 'That was me, boss,' he admitted.

'Really?' Red responded. 'But *they* didn't know that.'

After a significant pause, he added, 'I might have been seen.'

'What have I told you?' he screamed. 'Never when there's anyone watching!'

Dash gulped. 'Sorry, boss. I was hungry.'

Red sighed wearily. 'Be that as it may,' he continued slowly. 'It just proves our point. We have to catch the killer in the act. Then, they won't be able to argue.'

I nodded.

I just wasn't sure how we'd go about it.

We spent the best part of the next two weeks staking out the Tall Man's home and observing his movements. We gathered our intelligence and a pattern began to emerge. On Thursdays and Fridays he was out all day. The rest of the week, he was at home, although he left regularly on shopping expeditions. We came to the conclusion that he worked part-time, two days a week. If we were to do anything at his home, we had two days in which to do it.

The bad news was that the foxes reported him often going out late at night. It followed no regular pattern, but it was never more than three nights apart. On those occasions, they followed him and watched as he tried to lure cats into his range. Every time, he found a secluded spot and put food onto the ground and waited. Whenever cats were attracted, the foxes would let out an alarm bark and they'd take flight. For two weeks, thanks to the good work of the foxes, cats were safe. Throughout this period, the foxes never had to reveal themselves.

We could tell that our target was getting frustrated. We frequently heard ranting from inside the house, including several words that I hadn't learned from Lucy's books.

10

A Valiant Attempt

One morning at the crack of dawn, Dash paid me a visit. He was returning from his night-time vigil at the house. There had been no movement of the Tall Man. He told me that he and the foxes were growing weary of the surveillance. Some animals possessed impressive quantities of patience. Foxes were not one of them. Being generally nocturnal, they'd been responsible for the night shift. Throughout their weeks on patrol, no cat had been harmed. There had been near misses, but they'd carried out their duties commendably. However, their families were missing the food they'd normally bring back in the mornings. They needed to get back to hunting and scavenging.

I'd listened carefully to my elders. I want to make that quite clear. When Flash and Diamond had expressed their concerns regarding burning the killer's house down, there was a part of me that agreed with them. I knew it was against the law and I knew innocent animals might get hurt. I just couldn't think of any other way. If we could render his house uninhabitable, he'd have to move elsewhere. That would solve our problem, but like Flash said, it would simply transfer it somewhere else. If we could alert Cotton's police human to the danger, he could act. But how would we do that, why would he believe us and where was our evidence?

I waited until the next time I saw Digger in the garden. I told him I wanted to convene a meeting the following evening. Anyone who had an interest should attend, including the foxes. He would spread the word and ensure a decent turnout. That's if he didn't forget or give them the wrong information.

As it turned out, Diamond was the only one unable to attend. He was feeling a little under the weather. He claimed it must have been something he ate, but the rest of us ascribed it to old age. We could have used his caution and experience. Several cats and two mice I'd never met took their places noisily.

I was young, I couldn't help eyeing the mice greedily.

I'd seen meetings called to order in one of Lucy's books. The chairman invariably banged a gavel. I didn't have one. Everyone was talking at once. I let out a loud yowl. It was what I was best at.

'Order!' I shouted. Gradually, the level of noise diminished. Finally, there was silence. 'As you all know,' I began, 'we've identified the Tall Man and we've been keeping watch on his house for over two weeks.'

'Are there any snacks?' came a cry from Ginger at the rear. I'd forgotten he was there. We'd been seeing less and less of him every day. As things had become more dangerous, he was finding more pressing business elsewhere.

I sighed. Some people weren't taking proceedings seriously. 'No!' I replied. 'There are no snacks.' I took a deep breath and continued. 'Tomorrow is Thursday, the killer works on Thursday.'

Cheers rang round the crowd. Ally barked in appreciation.

'Why are you all cheering?' I asked.

Silence.

I shook my head. 'Tomorrow we will strike!' I said with emphasis. I waited for their agreement. I thought now was the time to cheer, but everyone was silent, looking up at me expectantly.

One of the mice asked something very quietly.

I didn't hear. 'Excuse me?' I prompted.

He repeated his question. I looked at him blankly. Secret, who was standing twitching beside him, relayed the message. 'Cheesy said, "How?"'

'How what?'

'How will we strike?' Secret explained.

'Right!' I wasn't looking forward to this bit. 'We're going to set fire to his house!' I cried with passion.

Again, everyone was very quiet. Some looked aghast. Flash shook her head sadly.

The little mouse was sitting in an upright position with his arms crossed. He didn't appear overly impressed. His mouth was moving again but I didn't hear anything. I looked hopefully at Secret. 'He said, "How will we do that?"'

'Okay, first we collect piles of dry leaves and sticks. Paper, if possible. Then we take it all around to his house.'

'How will we get in?' Ally barked.

'I'm glad you asked,' I responded smoothly. In fact, this was the part about which I was unsure. I'd only briefly seen the back of his house during my ill-advised excursion through the gate. 'I'm hoping that he leaves a window open,' I explained. 'Secret climbs up and scoots inside,' I informed them quickly.

'Excuse me!' Secret cried.

'He then unlocks one of the bigger windows and lets us all in,' I continued. It seemed quite straightforward to me.

'I...!' Secret responded with a loud gulp.

'Then we carry all the leaves and sticks inside, make a pile and light them with the fire stick.'

'Who's going to light the fire stick?' Flash asked incredulously.

'Secret will hold it and Ally will push the button.'

'Am I part of this?' Ally asked.

'We're all part of this,' I confirmed.

'Will it work?' Flash asked doubtfully.

'Ah!' I replied. 'I brought it along to try.' So saying, I galloped off and retrieved the fire stick from the shed, holding it unsteadily in my mouth. I dropped it on the floor in front of Secret. He settled down alongside the fire stick and held it with his grasping forepaws with the button facing upwards. Ally immediately bounded over and landed on the button with his right paw.

'No!' I cried, but it was too late. A jet of fire shot out of the tip, igniting the hairs of Secret's tail. He shrieked and ran off, leaving a lingering smell of burning squirrel hair. 'Well, that went well.' All eyes were on Secret, still running around the garden. The flames had been extinguished, but wisps of smoke still rose from his tail. Eventually, he returned to the group.

'Look at my tail!' he screamed.

We all took a look. There was a distinct semi-circular indentation, as if someone had taken a bite out of it. And it still smelled from the singed tips.

'So, is everyone clear?' I asked, ignoring Secret.

'When will we do this?' Flash asked.

'We'll all assemble tomorrow morning. He leaves for work early, so we'll take as much material to burn as we can carry. We'll find more when we get there.'

'What about all the security?' Flash asked.

'We should have enough time.'

'What about the parrot?' she persisted.

I hadn't worked that out yet. 'Maybe he won't be there,' I suggested.

She raised an eyebrow. 'You're right,' she nodded sarcastically. 'He could have arranged to go out with his friends.'

'We should let him out!' Ally said. 'He doesn't have to get hurt.'

'What if he has other pets?' Flash wasn't letting the matter drop. 'Are you going to rescue all of them?'

I looked at her blankly. 'Yes,' I replied uncertainly.

'Then it all depends on finding a way in,' she continued, doubtfully.

'Yes.' Finally, a question I could answer. I tried to wrap things up quickly. 'Any questions?'

'What happens if we get in and can't get out again?' Shadow asked.

I just looked at her. She was looking very beautiful. I invited any more questions from the assembled gathering and, when no-one asked anything, I went on, 'Finally, I've decided to give us a name.'

'Why?' someone enquired.

'Because we're like a club,' I explained. 'We should have a name.'

'What did you have in mind?' Flash asked dubiously.

'I was thinking of LADs: The London Animal Detectives,' I told them proudly.

'That's sexist!' she replied.

'Oh!'

'Wait!' cried one of the foxes. 'What about the London... Exceptional Animal Detectives?'

'LEADs,' I pondered.

Flash nodded enthusiastically. 'They're what humans put on dogs when they take them for a walk,' she explained.

'Yes,' I responded. 'I'm aware of that.'

'And!' she went on. 'They're what detectives try to find when they're solving crimes.'

'That's good!' I admitted. 'That's very good.' There was a general nodding from all around, coupled with an annoying murmuring.

One of the mice said something. I could see its lips moving. 'Secret?' I enquired.

'Hmm...' He seemed to be giving something his full consideration. 'Squeak says we should be called TAILs,' he said. 'It's quite appropriate.'

'What does that stand for?'

'The Animal Investigators of London,' he explained.

'That's awesome!' Dash cried.

I had to admit, it was a fitting name. We all had tails, although Secret's was looking a bit sorry for itself. 'Well done, Squeak!' I told him. 'It's a perfect name. Are we all agreed?'

More nodding confirmed the decision. 'Henceforth, we will be known as TAILs.'

Nobody else seemed to have any questions and, even if they had, I doubted my ability to answer them. I decided to adjourn the meeting. 'We'll meet again tomorrow morning!' I cried. It was supposed to be a rallying call, but everyone just turned and skulked away.

At least Shadow stayed.

*

The following morning dawned bright and sunny. I'd spent some time the previous evening scouting around for anything we could burn. I pulled a few scrunched up pieces of paper out of Lucy's wastepaper basket, but carrying them was going to be a problem. I could only manage one at a time. Maybe the killer would have some rubbish lying around. In any case, I had to bring the fire stick.

The turnout was the same as the previous day, although Dash and Creeper had been out all night and needed their sleep. They'd been replaced by two younger foxes: Russet and Gruff. We decided that the mice wouldn't be much help so we thanked them and left them behind.

We set off in convoy. Every animal was carrying something. Flash had managed to grab a small bag of wood shavings left over from an old hamster cage. They'd be excellent. She recognised that we were determined to do something and she wanted to come along to keep us out of trouble. That didn't mean she approved, of course.

Diamond was still absent with his mysterious illness. I hoped he was getting better, but he'd probably only slow us down. Anyway, we all knew he disapproved of our plan. Ally took the lead and guided us through the maze of streets. At one point, the two young foxes were lured away by the smell of food. I heard dustbins tumble as they tried to forage. When they returned, they were both licking their lips, so I imagine they'd had a snack. They also brought with them some greasy paper, presumably from a meal of fish and chips. That would burn well.

We reached the street and took up position in the front garden. We waited a suitable time to ensure that the Tall Man hadn't returned home. Everything was quiet. There was no sign of his bicycle. I looked up at the cameras, blinking regularly in our direction. I had no doubt we'd all be recorded on video as soon as we set foot on the drive. With any luck, the fire would damage the recording equipment.

I looked across at the senior of the two foxes, Russet, and asked, 'Coming?'

'Do we know if there's any security inside?' he asked.

'We're about to find out.'

He nodded curtly and we made our way to the gate. I could pass underneath with just a dip of the head. Russet had to squat and inch himself forward in a most ungainly manner. The birds started to shriek in their cages.

'Intruders!'

'Unauthorised access!'

'Call security!'

I looked up at them. 'Will you calm down!' I appealed.

'What is your business here?' the kestrel demanded.

'We're just going to have a look around,' I lied. 'Please keep quiet. You'll wake the Rottweiler next door.'

'I'll be reporting this incursion,' I was

warned. Thankfully, when they realised I didn't mean them any harm, they stopped complaining.

I shook my head looking at them. They should be flying in the countryside, free. Instead, their most pressing concern was when they were next going to be fed. I checked the lock on the aviary: it was a strange semi-circular affair with a rotating handle. I wasn't sure that we'd be able to open it, even if we wanted to.

I could smell the rotten odour of Rottweiler from over the fence. I didn't want to encounter him again. I reminded Russet to keep quiet. It wouldn't take much noise to wake him. I sat on my haunches and looked at the rear of the house. There was a single window open, a narrow horizontal one above a normal window. From my low trajectory, I couldn't see which room it was, but if it followed the layout of my home, it would be the kitchen. A drainpipe ran down the wall close enough to the open window for Secret to leap across. Unfortunately, it didn't come to the ground, turning horizontally and continuing around the corner.

'What do you think?' whispered Russet.

I looked at him. Then I looked at the drain pipe. 'How close can you get to the pipe with your front paws?'

Obediently, he moved to the wall and reached up with his front legs. When he was fully extended, he was within a couple of feet of the pipe. Of course, Ally was much bigger than Russet. I thought there was a good chance that Secret could make it to the pipe. 'This is going to work,' I told him.

'We need more than a squirrel inside,' he replied.

'He'll have to open the main window.' If he could open the larger window, we could all get in. I'd have no difficulty leaping up to the windowsill.

'How?'

'He has very strong fingers on his forepaws,' I explained.

'Strong enough to open a window?' he asked doubtfully.

I wasn't certain. 'We're about to find out. Wait here,' I instructed. I edged under the gate and called to the others. 'It's all clear! Come!'

They all trudged behind me. I watched as Ally struggled to get his bulk through the narrow gap. I hoped we wouldn't have to make a quick getaway. They all took turns admiring the aviary. Flash exchanged some pleasantries with the raptors, before moving on.

We lined up on the edge of the paved patio. We all chose to sit on the grass rather than the cold, uncomfortable stone. We didn't want to get piles. 'Firstly,' I addressed them quietly. 'No noise! The Rottweiler is sleeping next door. We want it to stay that way.' There was a chorus of nods. 'This is how it's going to work. Ally, you stretch as high as you can towards that drainpipe. Secret, you run up Ally's back and jump onto the pipe. Make your way along and leap over to the open window. Go through and open the main window. We'll join you inside.'

I thought my instructions were completely comprehensive, but I found Secret staring at me with an open mouth and disbelieving expression. 'What?'

'Is there a problem?'

'How do I get out again?' he cried.

'Shhh,' we all reminded him.

'You open the big window,' I repeated.

'How?'

I wasn't clear on that myself. 'It probably has one of those levers at the bottom. You'll have to lift it up off the pegs. Then the window will open.'

'How?' he repeated.

I took a breath. 'It opens outwards. Push it!'

'What if it's locked?' Flash asked.

'You find another window.'

Secret evidently wasn't happy with my plan. 'What are you going to be doing?'

'Helping,' I explained.

'Is that helping by doing nothing at all and leaving everything to the squirrel?'

'You have very strong fingers on your fore-paws,' Russet told him gruffly. 'You can do it.'

Secret sneered at him unpleasantly.

'I'm helping,' Ally pointed out.

'I have very sharp claws,' Secret told him.

Ally grimaced.

'Is everyone ready?' I asked.

'Everyone! Huh!' Secret scoffed.

Ally loped over and casually reared up on his hind legs, placing his forepaws perpendicular to the horizontal drainpipe. His shoulders were now at the level of the bend at the base of the pipe. 'You really want me to run up your back?' Secret asked earnestly.

'Yes, carefully!'

Secret moved several paces back and took a run up. He made steady progress, but it wasn't without pain. 'Ow! Ow! Ow! Ow! Ow! Ow! Ow! Ow!' Ally cried with every step. Secret's claws were exceedingly sharp! One more step on Ally's shoulders and Secret propelled himself onto the pipe. It was clearly slippery as his claws worked frantically to get a grip. Eventually, he settled down.

'Piece of cake!' he called, breathing heavily.

'No thanks, I'm on a diet,' the other fox, Gruff, responded.

'Can you get to the window?' I hissed.

He tried to stand but his claws kept slipping. Finally, he made his way to the vertical section. He was so close. He held on tightly. 'I can't climb this!'

'Try!' I urged.

Slowly, we watched as he edged up the pipe. He had to use the brickwork on one side to get a decent grip, the pipe was too slippery. We watched in admiration as he climbed higher. Then we watched in horror as he slid all the way back down, barely managing to hold on at the junction. He looked down at all our disappointed faces.

'Alright, alright!' he whispered and started the ascent again. This time he managed to reach up and grab one of the bolts holding the pipe to the wall. Balancing himself precariously, he took a breather.

'You can jump from there!' I called.

'Are you crazy?'

'Take a look. I've seen you jump further than that,' I told him.

He needed to get those strong hind legs anchored well enough to propel himself forward. There was a horizontal lever on the open window. He could reach that and grab hold. Then he could drag himself inside.

He managed to get his left foot on the bolt. He was going to try. I suggested to Ally that he should stand underneath in case Secret didn't make it. He could cushion his fall. I didn't want any fatalities on this mission. Secret appeared to be trying to convince himself that he could make the jump. He kept looking over at the lever and then glancing down at where he thought he might fall. I think he drew some comfort from Ally's presence. From where I stood, it didn't look too far, but I wasn't suspended in the air in danger of falling.

Finally, he settled down and stared at the crossbar. He seemed to be counting himself down. Then he leapt. He flew through the air gracefully and managed to hook his chin and forepaws over the lever. The rest of his body hung down loosely. Grappling for all his might, he pulled himself up and scooted through the open window. On the inside, he jumped down, landing on something midway up. Finally, his face appeared at the bottom of the window with a big grin. He said something in triumph, but the pane of glass prevented us hearing what it was.

He began to work at something at the base of the window. We all saw clearly as another lever was raised. He stood on his hind legs and pushed the glass. It swung open without difficulty. Standing on the windowsill, he bowed. 'Please, enter.'

Digger was first, flying through and disappearing. I jogged over and leapt up to the windowsill. 'Good work, Secret!'

Ally made a bit of a racket jumping in. His bulk managed to knock a beer glass to the tiled floor. It shattered on impact. Digger meanwhile was flying backwards and forwards collecting the leaves, twigs and papers we'd brought with us and making a pile in the living room.

I took a look around. As befitted such a disreputable, criminal, member of society, his house was a mess. He hadn't done any washing up for days and balls of dust lurked in hidden corners of the kitchen. The smell was unpleasant, not enough to make you want to run in the other direction, just unclean and somewhat fetid. I wandered along the hall and through to the front room. It was decorated in dark colours. All the furniture was dark wood. The curtains were full length dark fabric. They looked highly flammable.

The parrot had a cover on his cage. Presumably he was sleeping. I remembered what Flash had said, he was innocent. I watched as everyone got to work and jumped onto the arm of the sofa close to his cage. I reached up with my claws and pulled the cloth cover off. The bright daylight woke him immediately. He looked around in confusion. 'Who are you?' he asked in a loud squawk. 'What are you doing here?' His voice was grating, but I chose to ignore it.

'My name's Yowl. We are TAILs,' I told him proudly.

'Who? What?'

'The Animal Investigators of London,' I explained. 'Who are you?'

'They call me Travis.'

'Strange name,' I mumbled. 'We're here because the man who lives here, he kills cats.'

'No!' he cried. 'That's horrible!'

'Yes,' I assured him. 'We have to stop him.'

'What are you going to do?'

'We're going to set fire to the house.'

He was silent for a moment, casting his eyes

over the room, watching the activity. Everyone was helping to move the kindling to beneath the curtains. Digger was flying backwards and forwards, barely stopping for breath. They worked in silence. When they'd made a small pile, Digger gracefully landed and started scratching himself with his beak.

'Is that it?' I asked, disappointed.

'Yes!'

It didn't look very impressive. I was far from sure that even if we managed to light it, it would ignite the curtains. 'Have a look around,' I urged the others. 'See if you can find anything else, paper or wood.' I turned my attention back to Travis. 'We could let you out.'

'Yes, please!' he replied with a pleading look. 'I can help.'

'Really?'

'I know where there's some wood.'

'You do?'

'Yes.'

I wasn't certain I could trust him. Diamond's warning was ringing in my ears. His beak looked very sharp, but it was clear we needed more fuel for our fire. I decided I had to take a chance. 'Secret,' I called. 'Open the cage.'

He was busy sniffing round, looking for anything that would burn. 'What?'

'Open the cage.'

'OK.' He scooted over, climbed on the sofa, leapt onto the arm and jumped high in the air. His front claws hooked over the metal bars of the cage and he hauled himself up. I could only watch in wonder. He looked at the catch in confusion.

'Just pull it,' Travis instructed.

Secret locked his hind legs in place and pulled with the whole of his upper body. The catch disengaged. The door swung open with Secret still attached. 'Whee,' he cried swinging through the air. When he hit the cage, he dropped back down on the sofa.

Travis was already out and flexing his mighty wings. 'Over here!' he cried as he swooped down near the fireplace. He tapped three times on a strangely shaped metal container. 'Here.'

'Secret!'

He moved over with considerably less vigour than before, muttering, 'Always the squirrel!'

Once again, he released the catch without difficulty, Ally used his nose to open the lid. 'Wow!' he muttered. The container was stuffed full with a collection of thinly cut wooden sticks, ideal for lighting a fire. We all took turns collecting a stick or two and depositing them on top of the paper. We made a much more impressive pyramid. I was concentrating so hard, I failed to notice that Travis wasn't helping. That is, until he reappeared and picked up several sticks in his beak. He tried to look innocent.

'Err... Yowl,' Ally called from across the room.

'Hmm?' I replied with my mouth full of sticks.

'What's this?' His nose was behind the curtain. I couldn't see what he was pointing at.

I deposited my sticks on the growing pyramid and joined him behind the curtain. Close to the windowsill was a big red button. 'It's a big red button,' I told him.

'It's probably an alarm,' he suggested. 'Travis was behind here.'

'You think...?'

He nodded solemnly. 'We're going to have company.'

I looked at the pile of paper and sticks. It didn't reach up to the curtain but it would have to do. 'Let's get this done and get out of here.' We were ready for the fire stick. Ally fetched it in his mouth and laid it down, the business end close to the pile. 'Secret?' I called. He'd disappeared!

'Here!' came a call from down the hall. 'Have you tried these hazelnuts?' he asked casually.

'Cats don't eat nuts,' I told him.

'Shame!'

'Can you hold the fire stick?'

'Oh! Okay.' He bent down and held it in his forepaws. He pointed it at the base of the pyramid. This time he made sure his tail was well out of the way.

'Is everyone ready?' I asked. 'We do this and then we leave, quickly. Everyone?'

I received a chorus of agreement, so I nodded at Ally.

He reared up and let his weight fall on his right paw, smack on the button. A flame shot out and the greasy fish and chip paper immediately caught fire. We all watched as the flames grew, wrapping themselves around the wooden sticks.

Then there was a frantic pecking. I looked all around. It was coming from the ceiling. Travis was attacking a circular object in the centre of the room. His wings were flapping wildly as his beak crashed into the object time and again.

The base of the curtain was beginning to smoulder. As soon as I saw the first lick of flame on the material, I signalled everyone to leave. Our job was done.

It was raining!

Inside.

Hard.

I checked Travis. He'd gone. The small circular object on the ceiling was now spraying the entire area with water. Our smouldering pile was hissing and wisps of steam were rising from the ashes. Everyone galloped back into the kitchen, which was still mercifully dry.

I took a final look around the room and managed to locate Travis. He was standing on a bureau in a corner unaffected by the deluge, preening himself while staring in the mirror. He kept repeating, 'You talkin' to me? You talkin' to me?'

We reassembled in the kitchen. Secret's cheek pouches were so full of nuts he could hardly walk. He was the only one who seemed to have avoided a drenching. One by one, we all jumped down from the kitchen window. Digger flew out and alighted on the branch of a cherry tree in the garden. When everyone was out, we made for the gate.

'Cowards!' the kestrel cried.

'Retreating?'

'Withdrawing with your tail between your legs?' the osprey observed.

He was right. I quickly raised my tail to its normal, proud position. I tried to think of a fitting response. All I could come up with was, 'We'll be back.'

We squeezed under the fence and reassembled on the front lawn. It was all a bit of an anticlimax. We watched as the water continued to fall. All our hard work was ruined. Not only that, but he'd soon find out who was responsible. I was sure we'd all been captured on video.

We were startled by the rattling of a bicycle. We were all sitting there disappointed when the Tall Man rode up the gravel pathway. He must have been alerted by the alarm. Immediately, we were watchful. He saw us and jammed on the brakes, skidding over the gravel. We must have presented a motley collection, all drenched by the water. 'What the hell!' he shouted.

We all stared at him with hatred in our eyes. Slowly, one by one, we switched our attention from him to the deluge in his front room. He saw our attention wavering and turned and saw it for himself. 'Bloody hell!' he screamed. 'What have you done?'

He let his bicycle fall where it was and charged to the front door. He threw it open and raced inside. Within a minute, the cascading water had stopped. He drew his curtain back and raised the windows. It would take some drying out.

He stood there and glared at us. 'I'll get every single one of you!' he screamed. 'I know who you are!' Then he bent down and when he reappeared, he was holding a long weapon. It glinted in the sun.

'Time to go,' I muttered.

Noiselessly, we merged into the bushes and went on our way. We would all reassemble in Diamond's garden later. I thanked the two foxes and they made their own way home.

11

Diamond and Hewt's Plan

Later that afternoon, with the sun still high in the sky, we gathered again. The foxes didn't put in an appearance, but everyone else was there: everyone including Diamond, who never strayed too far from his bed. He looked old and tired, but whatever had confined him to his bed for the past few days was evidently improving. His steps were slow and uncertain. Flash never left his side.

'I understand,' he growled, 'that you *almost* succeeded in setting a fire in the killer's home.'

I stayed silent.

He shook his head sadly. 'First of all, I congratulate you on overcoming all the obstacles.' He took several deep breaths. 'However, I had advised against this course of action...' He left the implications linger. '*And* I warned you about the parrot.'

'We had to do something!' Shadow cried. 'He won't stop killing cats.'

Diamond nodded thoughtfully. 'Exactly why I spoke with Hewt this morning,' he told us.

I hadn't seen Hewt for some time. I wondered what they'd spoken about.

'Together, we've devised a plan.' He settled down deeper into his cushions.

'Plan?' I stuttered.

He looked in my direction. 'Junior, could you fetch the newspaper from the shed.'

I scuttled away and found the local paper folded neatly. The front page story was about the Tall Man and his ever increasing list of victims. I carried it in my mouth and placed it at Diamond's feet.

'Are you all listening?' he asked.

We all gathered round.

He proceeded to outline his plan in great detail. The pair of them had thought of everything.

The rest of us just needed to be ready.

I slept that night with one eye open. Actually, I'm not sure that's possible. What I mean is that I slept lightly. I was waiting for a signal.

It didn't come.

*

Diamond and Hewt's plan had sounded foolproof. It was both complex and extremely thorough. Contingency plans had been devised should any step in the process fail or diverge from its intended course. Everyone went away happy, including me.

The following morning, I wasn't so sure. My sleep had been interrupted several times, plagued by doubts. Over breakfast, I tried to explain my concerns to Shadow. She assured me that Diamond and Hewt had thought of everything and allocated their resources accordingly. We all had a role to play, some bigger than others. I grunted dejectedly in response.

I waited until she'd fallen asleep in the morning sun and went to visit Diamond. As always, Flash was by his side. Diamond was lying in his bed licking his lips as though he'd recently finished eating. He looked old and tired but I knew there was nothing wrong with his brain.

'Morning Junior,' he offered in a deep voice. Flash nodded a greeting.

'How are you feeling?' I enquired.

'Feeling?' He took a deep rasping breath. 'I feel like I'm coming to the end of a long distance race and I'm struggling to reach the finish line.'

Flash nudged his flank with her nose. 'There's plenty of life left in you yet.'

He regarded her with real affection in his eyes. 'Maybe.'

She laid down next to him, their bodies touching, their warmth shared.

'So, Junior. What can I do for you?'

'Well,' I started. 'I was thinking...'

'Good!' he interrupted loudly. 'You're learning!'

'Yes.' I wasn't sure how to begin. 'Your plan...'

'What about it?'

'Well, I don't seem to have anything to do,' I pointed out.

'Nothing to do!' he cried. 'You have the

most important job of all.'

'I do?'

'Of course!' he purred. 'Who else could we entrust it to?'

'Um...'

'We need someone reliable, trustworthy, diligent and brave. Can you think of anyone better?'

'I suppose...' I reflected. 'If you put it like that.'

'Naturally, we chose you!'

I felt honoured to be so highly thought of. I decided to be humble in acknowledging his praise. Then I had another thought. 'Wait!' I was in danger of losing my way amidst a labyrinth of flattery. 'What *is* this job that's so important?'

Diamond opened his mouth, a momentary doubt crossing his features. 'You're... our Production Manager,' he informed me smoothly. I suspected he'd made the title up. 'You're in charge of Quality Control.'

'Quality Control?' I queried.

'You are the coordinator. Your job is to oversee the entire operation. If anything's in danger of going wrong, you're responsible for resolving the problem. You'll have to think on your paws and allocate the resources at your disposal accordingly. It's a tough job.' He cast a glance at Flash, then returned to face me. 'Of course, if you don't think you're up to it.'

'No!' I replied hastily. 'If it's as important as that, I should definitely do it. I wouldn't want anything to go wrong.'

'Exactly!'

Flash looked up expectantly. 'Is there anything else?'

'Err...' I tried to think rapidly. I was in danger of being overcome by my own importance. 'No, I think that... Thank you for explaining.'

Diamond's eyes drooped shut. Flash gestured with her head that I should leave them alone. I didn't like the way Diamond was looking. I hoped he'd be back to his usual self before long.

I skipped away up the garden, feeling much better. As I squeezed under the fence, I heard a high-pitched chuckle. I froze and looked around. It had to be Secret but I couldn't see him. 'Where are you?' I demanded. I felt a sharp tap on my head, between my ears. He was hanging upside down on the fence immediately above me. He had a broad grin on his face. 'What's so funny?'

'You!' he cried, tears of laughter rolling down his cheeks. 'Diamond really pulled the wool over your eyes.'

'What are you talking about?'

'Production Manager! He just made that up.' He started laughing again.

'It's a very important job!' I explained, ignoring a suspicion that he was right.

'Very important as in, you have nothing to do!' I was beginning to get angry. He obviously didn't understand how pivotal my role was to the whole operation. He hadn't finished. 'He doesn't trust you! He thinks you'll do something stupid.'

'Nonsense! The entire plan is under my control.' He started to laugh again. I could feel my hackles rising. 'You think it's so funny, what's your job?'

'Ah!' he exclaimed with an air of self-importance. He hopped down to the ground and stood on his hind legs, his chest pushed out in pride. 'I've been made Communications Facilitator.'

I remained quiet for some time, digesting the news. 'Communications Facilitator?' I repeated. 'That's not a job.'

'It's very important,' he assured me. 'Without my input, there'd be no communications.'

'Right!' I was growing weary of his derision. Besides, I didn't want to disillusion him. He was evidently happy with the arrangements. I pointed my paw at an area beneath a distant oak tree. 'Is that an acorn?'

'Acorn!' he cried and disappeared at great speed.

I returned to my kitchen. I needed some fish biscuits.

*

Two days passed without incident. On the second, Shadow and I wandered over to take another look at the killer's house. The curtains were gone. Presumably he was going to replace them. Other than that, everything was unchanged.

Diamond continued his slow recovery and Shadow and I spent many hours in his garden with Flash. He was regaining his spirit, starting to smile again. He seemed happy, except when he remembered our breaking the law. He was still very disappointed that we'd ignored his advice, risked our lives and achieved nothing tangible. He was confident that his plan would bear fruit and nobody would get hurt. It was just a matter of time.

*

Well after midnight on the third night, my eyes suddenly opened. I'd been dreaming of chasing birds in the garden. In my dreams, I invariably caught them. In real life, I was still awaiting my first success. They were irritatingly quick. I looked around the kitchen wondering why I was awake.

Then I heard it again: an excited hoot from a high-flying owl. Suddenly, my brain switched into gear. I leapt down from my windowsill and scooted through the cat flap. I took a moment to get my bearings. I needed to know where Hewt was. Shadow came and joined me. We waited together with growing impatience. Then we heard it again. Immediately, we chased off in the direction from which we'd heard the call. I could vaguely hear Secret making his way down the tree trunk. Squirrels might have very short legs but they moved quickly across the ground.

Before we'd even reached the road at the front of our house, we heard an alarmed squawk, accompanied by an urgent flapping of wings. 'Ow!' We stopped in our tracks. It sounded like Digger. There was a series of rapid flaps, followed by a further, 'Ouch!' Then we heard a loud thud on the ground away to our right. 'Ow,' he groaned.

I had to take a decision. Hewt had obviously located the killer and, in the distance, I could hear the whoops of the foxes as they joined the chase. I turned to Shadow. 'Go on ahead. I'll be right behind you.' She turned to leave, Secret on her heels. 'Secret! You're with me.' He looked undecided. 'I might need some communications facilitating.'

'Ah! In that case...' He followed me in the

direction from which we'd heard Digger struggling. We found him under an apple tree, still groaning. 'What's the matter?' I asked urgently. Time was of the essence.

'It's not my fault!' he cried. 'I keep flying into things. I can't see in the dark. I'm not an owl!'

'Where were you going?'

'I have to get Ally. He's old and doesn't hear too well. I have to let him know.'

'Right!' It was obvious Digger couldn't negotiate all the trees in the garden. Things were going wrong. I had to think fast. Our carefully laid plan was already in danger of crumbling. 'Secret, go and... communicate with Ally.'

'Really?'

'Go! Now!' I urged. 'We need him!' He sprang away towards the back garden. 'Digger, you can stay in the shed at the back. We'll let you know what happens.'

'Right!' With a huge effort he managed to get himself airborne. As I raced in the direction of Hewt's increasingly anxious cries, I heard another loud thump. 'I'm alright!' came Digger's distant call.

I shook my head and continued to sprint. The two lead foxes, Dash and Creeper, were already out, coordinating with Hewt. I ran a long way, well beyond the Tall Man's house. Hewt contributed by keeping up the calls at regular intervals. Hopefully, we would all converge in the right place.

I could sense that I was getting closer, but I was faced with a crossroads and wasn't certain which route to take. I stood very still, waiting for the next cry. Instead, I heard the angry growl of a fox. It made me jump. I wouldn't want to be on the receiving end of an attack by an angry fox. We raced in the direction of the furious exchange. From a distance, we heard, 'Get off me!' in a high pitched voice. 'I'll make you wish...' Then I distinctly heard a yelp of pain. I tried to move faster.

Someone needed help.

Then I heard another fox. It could only be a fox. A loud, piercing wail. I took it as a sign of impending attack. Sure enough, the human uttered a harsh cry, accompanied by the sound of something metallic hitting the floor.

Suddenly, there were steps racing towards

me in the opposite direction. Cotton came into view, panting hard. 'Where's Ally?' she cried.

'He's running late,' I told her.

'He's supposed to wake up my human! He's a policeman.'

The sound of the fracas ahead was intensifying. The foxes wouldn't be able to hold the killer for long. He might still have a weapon. I didn't want any more casualties. I didn't know what to do.

'Anything I can do to help?' came a deep voice from the bushes.

'Red! It's good to see you. Can you bark?'

'Of course! I'm a fox.'

'Come with us.' I turned to Cotton. 'Lead the way!'

We weren't able to travel at full speed because Red was lagging behind. Before long, he was breathing heavily. 'Keep going!' he urged, but I could see his head was dropping.

'Is it much further?' I asked Cotton.

'Just around the next corner.'

'Come on Red. We're nearly there,' I encouraged.

'Not as young as I used to be,' he muttered

under his breath.

Finally, we drew up outside a modest house with a tasteful cream and white exterior. An adjacent street lamp illuminated the small front garden. Cotton stopped below a curtained window. 'That's his room, up there,' she informed us.

I turned to Red, who was lying on his side, gasping for breath. 'Red! We need noise.'

He already looked exhausted. He groaned and dragged himself to his feet. He took a deep breath, opened his mouth, and produced a pathetic, high-pitched yelp. He blew out his cheeks from the effort.

Cotton and I exchanged a worried glance. 'We're going to need more than that.'

His shoulders sagged. Finding some hidden inner strength, he stood up straight, pointed his head at the sky and produced an altogether more impressive effort.

'That's it!' I cried enthusiastically. 'More!'

Red continued his high-pitched barking and Cotton and I added our own agonised yowling. Together, we made an unearthly racket that resulted in several neighbours opening their windows and shouting at us. We all looked up expectantly at the bedroom window. Nothing stirred.

'More!' I encouraged, ignoring the protests of the local residents. 'Louder!'

We redoubled our efforts, increasing the volume. One of the neighbours threw something at us. I think it was a slipper. It missed, but not by much.

Eventually, a face appeared between the curtains. The window was pushed open. 'Cotton?' he called, trying to identify her in the gloom.

We continued the noise. Cotton started to race around in small circles, attempting to convey a sense of urgency. Her human looked puzzled: two cats and an elderly fox screaming in unison. It probably wasn't what he'd been expecting when he went to bed. The off-duty police officer shook his head and disappeared behind the curtains.

After several seconds, a light went on downstairs. We all sighed in relief and stopped the noise. I heard windows slamming closed along the street. When the front door opened, a very hesitant man in pale blue pyjamas enquired, 'What's the matter? What's going on?' He looked every bit the policeman: short, sensible hair and a sharp, vertical crease in his pyjama trousers.

Red wasted no time dashing forward and taking a mouthful of material just above his slippers. He pulled in the direction of the street, trying to get him to follow us.

'What?' he spluttered. He didn't appear too concerned having his leg pulled by a fox. When he didn't move, Cotton took his other leg and started to pull. 'Alright! I get the message.' He dipped back inside and emerged wearing his uniform jacket. After all, it was a cold evening. He grabbed his keys and his phone and shut the door behind him. 'Where to?'

We all dashed back into the road and headed for the confrontation, hoping the foxes had been able to hold the Tall Man. 'Wait!' we heard from a distance. We all looked at each other. Even at the moderate pace at which Red moved, we were still too fast for a human. This was going to take too long. I began to worry about the foxes.

Just then, Ally came sprinting into view, Secret riding on his back. 'Sorry I'm late!' he called out to us.

'It's alright. He's coming.' Then I had another thought. 'Ally, get to the killer as fast as you can. Help the foxes.'

'OK!' He raced back the way he'd come, Secret clinging on tightly.

We heard a car door slam and the engine start. Good! He'd be able to keep up with us in a car. We'd have to remember to stick to the roads. He wouldn't be able to follow us through the gardens. 'Tallyho!' I shouted and started to run. I'd read it in one of Lucy's books and it seemed appropriate.

We guided him back through the jumble of streets. His engine sounded uncomfortable travelling at slow speed. We turned a corner and I could smell blood. Someone had been hurt. I sprinted ahead, round another corner and was shocked by what I saw.

I recognised the Tall Man on his knees with each of his wrists being held firm in a fox's mouth: Dash and Creeper. One of the two younger foxes, Russet I thought, was lying on his side beside the pillar box. His brother Gruff had hold of one ankle and Ally the other. I guessed he'd arrived just in time. I made my way across to Russet. 'Are you alright?'

He nodded, but it was clear he was dazed. 'Collided with the red tower,' he explained.

I took a look around. I could see a knife where it had been dropped on the ground. A small cat was struggling to get up, although I couldn't see any wound. Shadow was with her. 'How is she?' I asked.

'Just winded,' she informed me. 'She was lucky.'

I nodded and returned to the killer. 'Well done Dash, Creeper,' I told them. Then I noticed that Creeper had a wound to his shoulder. It looked deep. I thought it could use stitches. He held on to the killer's wrist regardless of the pain.

'Alright!' the killer shouted. 'You've had your fun. Now let me go.'

Nobody moved a muscle. Then I saw Creeper's jaw tighten as the killer attempted to free himself.

'We can't stay here all night!' he screamed.

Gruff opted to disagree and took a hearty nip at the killer's ankle. He screamed in response. He wasn't going anywhere.

I was just responding to a sudden itch on my rear leg when I heard the siren of a police car. How appropriate! It was coming closer, travelling behind Red, who was staggering forward slowly.

We all waited as the siren drew nearer. The killer's demeanour had changed. Now he was frantically trying to break free. Russet struggled up, stepped closer and sank his fangs into his soft calf. The killer screamed again but stopped wriggling. They had the upper hand. Four foxes and an Alsatian against one human was no contest.

We heard a bark from nearby. Red eventually came panting round the corner and joined us. He collapsed on the ground trying to get his breath. The police car inched around the corner, carefully avoiding his prone body.

Cotton's police human stopped the car and climbed out. He looked very official in his policeman's jacket, pyjama bottoms and slippers. 'What have we here?' he asked no-one in particular.

Just then, Hewt swept down and landed alongside the prisoner. He had in his talons the local paper. He took great pains to lay it flat with the lead story visible. It was the latest instalment of the Cat Killer Chronicles. Satisfied, Hewt took off and landed on the nearby pillar box.

'The Cat Killer?' the policeman asked. Then he saw the knife. 'Is this the Croydon Cat Killer?'

We all frantically nodded in agreement.

'And what's this?' he asked, stooping to examine the knife. While his back was turned, he saw Tinker, lying quite still, breathing heavily. He walked across and bent down. 'Poor little thing! We'll get you some help.'

He walked to his car and took something out of the glove compartment. He emerged with a pair of handcuffs dangling from his finger. 'I think I'll take over from here, lads,' he told the foxes. Dash released his right hand and the handcuff was swiftly applied. Creeper repeated the process and the killer was secure. 'Looks like he's had a go at you too,' he muttered, noticing Creeper's bleeding shoulder.

After his prisoner was handcuffed, he withdrew an evidence bag from his jacket pocket. Carefully, he picked up the knife and placed it inside. 'Looks like we have blood on the blade and fingerprints on the handle,' he informed the killer. 'Should be enough to charge you and see you before a judge.'

He returned to his car and called for assistance on his radio. Then he came back holding his mobile phone. 'I think we should record this for posterity,' he told us. 'Gather round everyone.'

With the prisoner kneeling in the middle, we all lined up on both sides. Two foxes stood either side of him, me and Shadow one side with Ally behind, Flash, Cotton and Secret the other. Ginger had appeared out of nowhere and skulked at the rear. Red lay panting at the front. 'Hey!' the policeman cried to Hewt. 'You don't want to miss out!'

With a loud cry, we were joined by Hewt, who stood proudly in front of the group. We all smiled for the camera and there were three flashes of light. We were going to be famous. The policeman came and kneeled in front of us. 'Nice work, all of you. You caught yourself a villain. Well done.' He nodded to each of us in turn. 'Now, I think you'd better be getting back to your homes. If you want copies of the photo, ask Cotton. I'll print some up.'

With an angry yowl, we all wandered away from the killer. We heard another car pull up and watched from the shadows as he was loaded into the back seat. Hopefully, he wouldn't be allowed out for a long time after his trial.

Shadow, Flash and I stopped in Diamond's garden on the way back. We thought he should be the first to know that his plan had succeeded. He was fast asleep and we chose not to wake him. It could wait until the morning. Shadow was still sleeping in the shed and so I said goodnight. I dropped off Flash and hopped over the fence to my garden.

As I circled round trying to get comfortable on the windowsill, I thought about the events of the previous weeks. I'd been new to the area; I was welcomed with open arms by all the neighbouring animals; we learned of a danger; we formed an unlikely alliance with the foxes; I climbed the highest tree in the area; I flew through the air on the wings of an owl; I found a mate; we almost set fire to a house; and we captured a criminal.

All in all, not a bad few months.

THE END

Epilogue

Today marks the first anniversary of our capture of the Tall Man.

I know because the local paper printed the policeman's photo again. For a while, we were famous. Not that anybody knew who we were or where we lived, of course. The papers had been full of the story for weeks. International news channels sent reporters to our streets. None of them managed to catch sight of any of the protagonists. We were all keeping a low profile. They got our name wrong too. They always referred to us as *The Animal Detectives*. We'd have to put that right the next time.

The Tall Man slowly made his way through the legal system. He was found guilty and received a short prison sentence. We were all disappointed, we'd been hoping for several years. Apparently, animals are not valued as highly as humans. The police were warned to watch him when he was released. We would too! It was not what we'd hoped for, but better than nothing.

Life went on very much as normal.

The morning after his arrest, Digger alerted us to unusual activity at the killer's house. We all chased over there and watched from a distance as the RSPCA carefully rounded up his birds and took them away in a van. I read in the local paper that they would be re-housed at a bird sanctuary in the north. Every effort would be made to teach them survival skills with a view to releasing them into the wild. Perhaps one day they'd feel the sun on their backs and the wind on their feathers. They might also experience the dubious pleasures of catching and eating small rodents. Maybe they'd even grow to enjoy it.

One day, Lucy's mother returned from her part-time job with a smile on her face. She'd paid a visit to the vet and he'd recommended a course of treatment for the fleas that had made my bed so uncomfortable. It was my first time swallowing a tablet. It tasted disgusting, but it seemed to do the trick, for a while.

Diamond didn't survive the year. We all showed our appreciation of his excellent plan, although he insisted that Hewt was equally responsible. His illnesses grew more and more frequent. Two visits to the vet suggested that little could be done. He was just getting old. Flash spent more and more time by his bedside and was inconsolable for a while after he died. It all happened very peacefully. He was sleeping and simply didn't wake up.

His owners were similarly broken-hearted and replaced him with a Siamese. Hmm... She's a bit stand-offish and doesn't like to engage too much with the neighbours. We all miss Diamond.

The morning after we caught the killer, I confronted Diamond. There was something I didn't understand. I wanted to know why he'd selected Digger to alert Ally when he must have known he couldn't fly in the dark. He replied mysteriously, 'I've known Digger for more years than I care to remember. I know *exactly* what he's capable of.'

'Then why did you choose him?' I asked.

'He was the right one for the job,' he told me with an enigmatic grin.

I couldn't get anything else out of him. Like everyone else, I was devastated when he died.

We also lost Digger. He disappeared. No-one knows what became of him. He'd always been willing to help, although sometimes his memory let him down. I haven't given up hope that one day, he'll return. There's now a dove that spends time in the garden, Clover we call her. If we need to know what's going on, she always keeps up to date with the local gossip.

Ginger also departed within a few weeks of our triumph. His family moved to the seaside. We all wished him well. For us, the smart-talking, perpetually youthful, streetwise cat would never grow old. He was a character, even though we pushed the limits of his bravery beyond what he was comfortable with.

The morning after the arrest, Shadow and I paid a visit to Red and the foxes. We could never have managed without them. They were the real reason we'd managed to catch the Tall Man. Red invited us into their den and we had a long conversation. Creeper was confined to his bed, but his wound already showed signs of healing. He deserved a rest. The others could look after him until he was back on his feet.

As we were going, I asked Red a personal favour. 'Do you think it would be alright if, some mornings, I came over and played in the garden with the cubs?'

'I wish you would!' he replied. 'I'd be delighted. It would be good for them.'

As we said goodbye, he touched me nose to nose. That is a sign of great respect in the world of the foxes.

Every week I try to make an effort to get up early and pay a visit to the cubs. It's a joy to watch them frolicking with the youngest generation of cats and squirrels. I'd go more often but they wear me out. We play with them and try to teach them the ways of the world. In the absence of Diamond, I've taken responsibility for passing on words of wisdom and caution. My impetuous youth is behind me, almost. I've matured. I'm always ready to listen to tales of woe and attempt to find a solution.

And the best part of all, we cats are safe at nights again.

Coming soon...

TAILs II
Yowl & the Fugitive from Justice

Just below the report of our success catching the Tall Man, was an article about a local pedigree dog who'd gone missing. It was interesting because it was just the latest in a number of similar cases. Dognapping was big business and a growing problem. The perpetrators sold the stolen dogs to new owners for substantial sums of money. Dogs had gone missing from homes, gardens and even cars. This was becoming a serious issue.

I made a mental note to talk to Flash about the dognappers. My mind was already working. Maybe there was something TAILs could do about it...

Fight, Maria, Fight!